A VERY SCOTCH AFFAIR

Robin Jenkins (1912–2005) studied at Glasgow University and worked for the Forestry Commission and in the teaching profession. He travelled widely and worked in Spain, Afghanistan and Borneo before finally settling in his beloved Argyll. His first novel, *So Gaily Sings the Lark*, was published in 1951 and its publication was followed by more than thirty works of fiction, including the acclaimed *The Cone-gatherers* (1955), *Fergus Lamont* (1979) and *Childish Things* (2001). In 2002 he received the Saltire Society's prestigious Andrew Fletcher of Saltoun Award for his outstanding contribution to Scottish life.

ROBIN JENKINS

A
Very Scotch
Affair

Polygon

For Mary Wiseman
who may remembera promise
made in a far-off Keningau

This edition published in Great Britain in 2005 by
Polygon, an imprint of Birlinn Ltd
West Newington House
10 Newington Road
Edinburgh
EH9 1QS

www.birlinn.co.uk

First published in 1968 by Victor Gollancz Ltd

ISBN 10: 190459844 7
ISBN 13: 978190459844 2

Scottish
Arts Council

The publishers acknowledge subsidy from the
Scottish Arts Council towards the publication of this volume.

British Library Cataloguing-in-Publication Data
A catalogue record for this book is
available on request from the British Library

Typeset by Hewer Text (UK) Ltd, Edinburgh
Printed in Denmark by Nørhaven Paperback A/S

PART ONE

I

"THE TROUBLE WITH you, Mungo, is that you're too Scotch. You enjoy letting your conscience torment you. You're out-of-date."

The harshness of the words, delivered with her schoolmistressy deliberation, did not quite, it seemed to him, conceal the very Scotch kind of respect underlying them. Tears of gratitude almost came into his eyes; but mawkish self-pity was another Scotch failing, and he did not have the usual excuse of drink. He tried to make his pressure on her thin cold hand manly as well as loving.

"Adultery," he repeated, shaking his head.

The mean arid word disintegrated in his mind and lay scattered there like the crumbs on this and adjacent tables. Through the tearoom window he could see the sleet streaming in the lamplight out of the dark January sky, and people, muffled up under umbrellas, hurrying for bus and train. The few other customers, crouched over their cups, looked as if their tea, bodies, and consciences alike, were tepid and weak. At the cash desk the buxom woman patted her frizzy pink hair and yawned. Even her admiration of him as a big handsome man had inside quarter of an hour turned stale as a neglected cake.

"Adultery," he said, for the third time.

Myra said it too, with her thin lips only; sneered and shrugged her shoulders.

"It's an ugly word," he muttered.

"Why keep saying it then?"

He nodded: why indeed stay imprisoned within the

mentality and standards of what Peggy his eighteen-year-old daughter called the ghetto, that working-class area of tenements in which he had lived all his life?

He tried to laugh. "You know, Myra, when I was a wee boy, about eight or nine just, I remember asking my auntie Kirstie what it meant."

"The ragwoman?" Herself the daughter and granddaughter of doctors, she always professed to be amused by the thought of his dead old aunt, his foster mother. "She that wore a man's cap and carried a bag on her back, and blew a bugle in the streets?"

"Aye, her."

"It was a stroke of genius being brought up by her."

He noticed no irony. He just thought here was the difference between Myra, intellectual and emancipated, and his wife Bess who, if ever there was one, was a creature of that ghetto. For instance, an ex-carpet factory worker herself and the daughter of a plasterer's mate, she was nevertheless so stupid a snob that she had dared him to tell the children about his upbringing in the ragstore. Yet she had a local reputation as a humorist, and had found reasons to laugh at his war reminiscences in which comrades were blown to bits.

"But, Mungo, you were surely very precocious to have asked such a question at that age?"

"Well, I'd been given the Commandments to learn by heart, you see. I didn't understand what this word adultery meant. It worried me."

"It would."

"So I decided it must mean cheating at rounders."

"Rounders?"

"Yes. There was a word we used for a base at rounders: dult."

"I can't say I ever heard it."

"You were brought up in avenues, not streets. It was our

8

word. Well, we cheated often enough, I suppose, refusing to be out, or not waiting till the ball was struck, and so on."

"I'll never believe you cheated, Mungo."

Again he did not notice the irony, though this time it was almost mockery. He was too intent on staring back at the lonely anxious child he had been. "Not often. Not as often as the others. I was too scared."

"Scared? Never. Too honourable, you mean."

He nodded: yes, he had always been too honourable to cheat, bully, lie, and deceive. Even during that vast opportunity the war he had not succumbed as readily as most. Though it had been looted shamefully from an old terrified woman the German silver eagle on the mantelpiece at home represented no boast but rather was a reminder of how much he and the rest of the world had to make amends for. Yet for his pains Florence McTaggart, Bess's friend, regarded him as a monster of selfishness and duplicity; and Bess just laughed.

"And what did your comic auntie tell you adultery was?"

He was very earnest. "She just smiled and put her hand on my head. Is it still there, Myra? I can feel it."

His hair, prematurely silvered, was always well cared for. She amused herself imagining it desecrated by an old smelly, wizened, dirty, female paw.

"I was the bright scholar, she said, not her. What did I think it meant? So I told her, cheating at rounders. She said very likely I was right, that's all it meant."

Myra lit another cigarette. He did not smoke.

"Well," she said coolly, "in certain circumstances it's no worse. If people love each other truly, who can say they're doing wrong, who has a right to condemn them?"

The very hairs in his moustache tingled. It always thrilled him that Myra, refined, cultured, intelligent, and well-off, should be so much franker in talking about love than fat, gluttonous, unimaginative, and, in the dark, lecherous Bess.

9

"As I've said before, Mungo, your wife degrades you."

Yes, it was true, Bess did degrade him, wilfully. All their married life she, who never read a book herself, had sought to stultify his every intellectual ambition.

"Your children will go their own ways soon enough. Why sacrifice yourself any longer on their account? They certainly won't thank you for it. Yes, Mungo, the time's come when you must escape."

Yes, but Myra too did not quite appreciate the complexities of the trap he was in; like Bess she was inclined to disregard his ideals.

"Listen to this," he said, and dragging the damp *Glasgow Herald* from his raincoat pocket opened it at the page where the letters to the editor were.

"We're talking about us, Mungo, not reading newspapers."

"This is really about us, Myra; well, about me anyway."

"What is it?" she snapped.

"It's a letter about this new housing estate at Carmunnock."

"For heaven's sake, we're not going to live there. I'd rather have one of your slums."

He was disconcerted. "You can't mean that, Myra."

"Yes, I do mean it. But go on, read whatever it is you want to read."

"All right." But he read rather huffishly and she did not pay much attention. " 'No doubt I shall be accused of antisocial tendencies, but as the owner of one of the original houses in the village of Carmunnock, soon to be engulfed by this enormous housing estate projected by the Corporation, I would like someone to tell me this: Who is going to compensate me, and others in my position, for the drastic reduction in the value of our property that will inevitably ensue.' "

"Sensible enough," commented Myra. "Though I still don't see what it's got to do with us."

"But, Myra, can't you see I would like to be in a position to tell him, and everybody like him: Your compensation is simply that the value of humanity is raised by taking people out of slums and putting them into decent houses where their minds can get a chance to blossom. That's what I would like to be able to tell him."

"Well, why can't you? What's preventing you?"

He shook his head and frowned.

"Is it our adulterous relationship?"

"Don't put it that way, Myra."

"That's the way your eyes are putting it at this moment, Mungo. It's the way they put it too damned often."

"I do not like deception."

She smiled. "I don't think you mind as much as you think you do, Mungo. But supposing it's true, why not stop it? Why not tell your wife about us?"

"It's not only her. It's the children too."

"Tell them. Break with the lot of them honestly."

"Honestly?"

"Yes, honestly. You owe me something too, you know. In a fortnight's time I leave for Barcelona. You've seen Ethne's letter. Didn't she make life there sound a lot brighter and happier than it ever could be here?"

He nodded. Inwardly he said that Ethne in her letter had sounded like a whore. She was a teacher friend of Myra's who had gone off to Barcelona years ago to earn a living teaching English.

"Well, aren't you coming with me?"

"As God's my judge, my dear, there's nothing I'd like better."

"Leave the piety out of it, please. And don't moan about your children. They're not children any more."

Andrew, at University, was twenty-one. Peggy was in the sixth form. Billy, though, was only twelve. He said so.

"Yes, but isn't he his mother's boy? Aren't they all on her side?"

It was astonishingly and dismally true. They all were, including Peggy. Yet it was he who had insisted on their getting a full education. Bess had grumbled that Andrew would be happier as a bank clerk, and would earn money all the sooner. It was he who had bought them the twelve volumes of the *Children's Encyclopaedia*; Bess had objected to the expense.

"I've never met your family, Mungo, and I never will, but it seems to me, from what you've told me, that they've combined, deliberately, to keep you down. But for them you would have been far more today than an insurance superintendent."

Surely that was true. He touched his moustache. In any company he looked distinguished, with his silver hair, his good skin, his fine build, and his handsome intelligent face. He could have been taken for an ex-Brigadier, though he had risen no higher than a sergeant. It was undeniable that Bess had kept him down; indeed, she boasted about it. A good wife, she claimed, saw to it that her man never went out without a clean shirt, brushed hair, and polished shoes; but it was still more important that he should never be allowed to appear in public with a self-esteem as foolish as a hat too big. The children had been her allies. Andrew and Billy used banter, often as wounding as impudence. Peggy used silence.

"Here's the chance you say you've been waiting for for years. Are you going to take it?"

Living with Myra, especially in a sunny city like Barcelona, his idealism would flourish. What a pity, though, she was not in body as soft, rounded, and loving as, say, little Nan Fraser who lived in the flat above, or, to be fair, as Bess in the first years of their marriage.

"Well, Mungo?"

"Myra, to go with you to Spain would be like entering into the promised land."

"It's as easy as buying an air ticket."

He winced at that insinuation about money.

"Break with them, Mungo. This very night."

"It's snowing." The excuse, as childish as any of Billy's, was out before he could stop it. "I mean, Peggy's got a bad cough. She was seeing the doctor today. I'd like to know what he said."

Myra grinned and blew smoke contemptuously towards him. "Tomorrow then."

"Yes, by God, tomorrow. Nothing will stop me." He laughed, rejoicing at the prospect of telling Bess. Let her laugh then if she could. Let Andrew and Billy sneer. Let Peggy keep her peace.

"You'll tell them tonight?"

"Yes, tonight."

"You swear it, on the honour of Mungo Niven?"

She grinned and he tried to grin back. "Yes, I swear it."

"It shouldn't come as much of a surprise."

That showed Myra did not understand, probably never could be made to understand. The truth was he might well wear out his determination in his efforts to convince Bess he meant it. More than likely she would call on the children to laugh with her, at a threat that really was, so she would say, their father's Glasgow way of saying how much he loved her and depended on her.

After tomorrow too came Wednesday, a working day. Would Myra go off to school as usual, and he to his office? Bitterly he remembered one of Bess's remarks: "Working folk, wi' regular jobs and hames, juist don't hae time for hanky-panky."

"That's settled then, Mungo?"

"Settled once and for all, Myra."

13

"Good. Why should we let sleet and cold winds and sour faces spoil what should be the happiest time of our lives? Lovers deserve sunshine and blue skies."

His heart leapt. During the war he had served in Italy and had never forgotten that relaxation in the sun, of body and soul. He remembered great statues of men and gods with their privates as magnificently carved as their faces. Glasgow men in his company had been shocked, though they had shown it by the lewdest of blasphemies. He himself had felt grateful to the sculptors dead hundreds of years, to the contemporary Italians who daily accepted such stark magnificence, and to the blue sky above those curly stone heads. Some of that gratitude came warmly back to him now.

But the unrelenting morality of his native Glasgow could not be shaken off. "I'll still be financially responsible for them," he muttered.

Her voice was quick and sharp. "I've never suggested otherwise."

"If I give up my job I won't have a penny."

She, on the contrary, would have plenty. Her parents, both dead, had left her thousands.

For half a minute or so she smoked, with her eyes closed, as if doing mental arithmetic.

"We'll allow them," she said at last, slowly, "twenty pounds a week, for three months to begin with. After that, we'll see."

"But it would be your money, Myra."

"It would be, Mungo. It would have to be, wouldn't it?"

Miserably he nodded.

"All right then."

"If I don't go I think I'll start falling to pieces like a tree dead at the roots."

"Together we'll nourish those roots."

As he smiled rather furtively at her he wondered what she was defying or running away from. He knew so little about her.

14

2

IN THE BUS Mungo found himself hungry for assurance. Beside him snuffled indomitably an old man wrapped up in a thick damp overcoat and a green camphorated scarf wet with slavers. Outside, Glasgow might be dark and cold but its citizens, even the aged to whom the long grim northern winter was death, were the most approachable, warm-hearted, and generous-minded folk on earth.

He could not quite confide in the old fellow about Myra; it would have to be done more obliquely.

"Inclement night," he said.

"Murderous."

Mungo smiled: the reply was so realistic and yet so humorous too.

"Yet out in the country," he urged, "the snow will be bonny on the hills and trees."

The old man snarled.

"Not so far away either. Out at Carmunnock, for instance, where this big new housing scheme's being built that's to be an example to the whole world."

"Costing millions."

Mungo laughed. "Money well spent, though."

"Putting us in debt for generations to gie luxuries to scruff that'll appreciate them nae mair than pigs."

Eliminating the sourness, provoked by pain perhaps or merely by senile exhaustion, Mungo applauded the pithiness. "I wouldn't just say that," he replied. "I'd prefer to put it this way: the value of humanity is being raised. And that's the only kind of progress worth having."

"Progress? Is that whit you ca' it? Let me tell you, mister, I've been a ratepayer for ower fifty years wi' nothing to show for it at the end but a room and kitchen wi' an ootside lavatory for ten folk that last week was strangled wi' ice. Are you asking me in the name o' progress to subsidise bathrooms wi' tiled walls for scruff that'll spend mair on drink in a night than I can on food for a week for me and my auld wife? Progress? Murders and wars and robberies and strikes. Every winter I get inflamed kidneys. I hae them noo, at this very minute. Even if I had a private pan o' my ain it would be nae pleasure to pass water. Am I supposed then to listen to every fool's blethers aboot progress? Rabbie Burns was right when he said: Man, mind thyself. Share an ootside lavatory and you'll find oot how right he was; and the youngest are the worst. But this is where I get off, thank God."

Irascibly he struggled out of his seat, beating off Mungo's offer of help, and staggered to the exit.

Mungo tried not to feel discomfited or discouraged; or angered by the smirks on the faces of other passengers who had overheard. All that had happened was that one Glasgow man, middle-aged, vigorous, and optimistic, had had a friendly disagreement with another, a little less hopeful owing to old age, sickness, and ill luck. Especially tonight, Mungo was not so simple-minded as to think all was concord and comfort in his native city. Was not this Carmunnock project itself really a belated atonement for the notorious slums? Were not the Rangers and Celtic Ne'erday matches ill-famed throughout the civilised world for the savagery of the spectators, inspired by depraved religion? Were there not still some districts, one of them a few streets from his own home, where youths with bestial faces slashed each other with razors? And had not the University students, his own son among them, not so long ago pelted with soot and flour the luminary of the Government whom they had elected to be their Lord Rector? Indisputably Glasgow men could be violent, cantankerous, and thrawn. The city regiment, the Highland Light Infantry, in which he had served during the war, had demonstrated its ferocity in many countries. They could also be tender, even if too many of them needed a half bottle of whisky and a song like 'The Bonnie Wells o' Wearie' to make them show it. But they were all the time, in winter and summer, in ferocity and tenderness, in ease and hardship, in youth and age, generous-minded; within human limits naturally, which was the only qualification he was prepared to make.

"Stop kidding yourself, Dad," Andrew would say. "Glasgow's all right, but it's nothing special. Nowhere's special. When it's being let flourish sure it feels friendly; when it isn't, it doesn't. Same with everywhere else."

"Don't mind him, Mungo," Bess would cry. "How can you help being Glesca's spokesman, wi' such a name? When they christened you they saddled you for life wi' the city's responsibilities. There should be a statue of you in George Square. I believe you think there is, from the way you stand yonder and look up."

She would laugh till her big belly wobbled.

His colleagues in the small insurance company, the Royal Thistle, often chaffed him about his devotion to Glasgow; but he was well aware that the collectors, those thick-soled climbers of as high as Everest every week, over their chipped cups of tea in cafés tried to define to their satisfaction just what kind of a twister he was.

When he went out on to the platform of the bus he noticed there, among the three or four waiting to get off, little Nan Fraser. She was about thirty-two, demure and bonny, with a soft deliciously rounded figure. Often he lay at night beside Bess thinking of Nan in the arms of her feeble-brained Alec, a sorter in the Post Office.

"Oh, good evening, Mr. Niven," she said. "I never noticed you."

He was sure she had, though; it was because she'd caught sight of him inside that she had fled upstairs.

"Isn't this awful weather?" she said. "My Alec says Glasgow's not fit for human habitation from December to March, and on a night like this I think he's right."

Pushing against her, he felt the softness of her little buttock, and yearned to be her Alec, privileged every night to fondle it. Then, horrified, he ordered lust down and to help drive it away called up that faithful watchdog, his loyalty to his children. But tonight it was not at home.

So far there had been little sexual solace in Myra. Thin and bony, with small breasts, she directed their love-making so that she anyway got some pleasure out of it, whatever happened to him. As for Bess, when young, with a lovely exciting body, she had been cruelly mean about letting him see it. Now when it was unsightly she would stand right in front of him and yawn in the nude for a minute at a time, without bothering even to cover her mouth.

God knew he looked for nothing fancy in a woman of forty-six who had borne three children. He did not expect her to tint or dye her hair, but was there any need for it to be always so drab and untidy? She said she couldn't afford hairdressers, slimming biscuits, expensive girdles, and flattering clothes, as well as a son at University and a daughter in the sixth form. That was all true enough, but surely she should have learned, in her twenty-four years of marriage to him, that the truth ought never to be used as a skulking-place? Then in her almost revengeful deterioration she had taken to leaving out her false teeth at night, because, so she claimed, keeping them in gave her inflamed gums. Those shrunken kisses in the dark, demanded so coyly, had revolted him more and more. They were made worse too by her recounting, with inane mumbled laughter, some trivial gossip of house, street, shop, or whist-table.

So tenderly that it made her giggle, with annoyance as well as embarrassment, he helped Mrs. Fraser to alight and step across the gutter heaped with slush. The sleet was turning to snow.

"Goodness, Mr. Niven," she said, as she put up her umbrella, "you must be glad you're not out in your wilds on a night like this."

She called them his wilds because more than once he had amused her and Alec by telling them how he would like to live in the country, with trees round his house.

"I've just been thinking the opposite, Mrs. Fraser," he said earnestly. "It'll be quiet and beautiful out there. The snow will lie. Have you ever seen anything more beautiful than a tree with snow on it?"

She giggled again. Alec called him Niven the Poet, because he was always setting himself up as a judge of beauty. He had written to the *Glasgow Herald*, urging that as many trees as possible should be spared at Carmunnock where the new housing scheme was being built. Half a dozen letters had followed, actually supporting him. She pictured those trees this night, their sap frozen, their branches bare: did they know, as the snow settled on them, that they probably owed their lives to this big pompous fraud (another of Alec's names for him), born in a Bridgeton slum miles from any bush far less a tree?

All the same, as Alec said, no wonder he praised the beauty of trees. Certainly he couldn't very well praise the beauty of his wife.

"It's on a night like this, Mr. Niven," she said, "that we appreciate cheeriness like your Bess's."

The praise was to test his reaction. It was a game she and Alec played. They had already established that Niven was ashamed of his amiable slug of a wife, but Alec went further, he was convinced it had come to hate.

Reaching the tenement of red sandstone in which they both lived, in one of the pockets of respectability, they paused outside the clean well-lit tiled close while Mrs. Fraser put down her umbrella. As Mungo watched her he saw the snow glittering on his moustache in the lamplight. He felt inspired then above the tawdry longings of lust. It was not just a pretty face he saw, and a body on which assuagement might be found, but a fellow human being who no doubt had temptations and disillusionments of her own. Married seven years, she still had no family. Perhaps that was intentional, but it was possible that when she wanted a child conception would not happen, and she would be left all her life with only her Alec, whose head would grow balder and his wits thicker, and whose parsimoniousness, at present tolerated as thrift, would become despised as meanness.

She was laughing. It was rude but she could not help it: he looked so peculiar with his eyes squinting and doleful.

She had to fib. "I'm thinking of poor old Mrs. Gallie," she whispered, as they passed that lady's door. "She's dying, you know; but then she's seventy-eight. When I looked in yesterday to see how she was, do you know what was worrying her? She was afraid old Knox, her cat you know, would fall into Papish hands, as she put it herself."

As she spoke Mrs. Fraser was remembering that Mrs. Niven was far from pleased that her Andrew, the University student, on whom she doted, was going about with a Catholic girl who worked in a grocer's.

Niven did not seem to be listening. He was far away among his snowy trees. "Not only are trees beautiful," he said, "they have no decisions to make."

They had reached the landing on which he lived.

"Well, I'd better get away up," said Mrs. Fraser. My

goodness, she was thinking, just wait till Alec hears about the trees that have no decisions to make. "I'm a bit late tonight. Alec will be wondering what's happened to me. Good-night, Mr. Niven. Give my regards to Bess."

"I shall do that. And give mine to Alec."

"Surely." And when she did Alec and she would yell with laughter at the man's impertinence. Decisions! You would think he was the manager of the insurance company and not just a promoted collector. If he had had money his presumption, and his appearance, might have been pardoned; but he earned a good deal less than she and Alec combined. Or if he had been in a position of authority, like an M.P. or even a councillor. As it was, he had been born in Culdean Street, still today one of the scruffiest in the east end, and had been brought up by a half-mad old aunt said to have been a rag-dealer. What possible right had he to think himself important? His son Andrew was at University true enough, but only by the skin of his silly-looking teeth, and he would more likely than not fail in his final examinations. As for Peggy, his favourite, said to be brilliant, well, she was no doubt clever enough, but her school, Riverbank Senior Secondary, hadn't anything like the standards of a fee-paying one like Hutcheson's or the Girls' High. There the dux of Riverbank would be lucky to get into the first twenty. Besides, with her ban-the-bomb badge, beatnik hair, and thin, freckled solemn face, she was trying to be too original for her family's station in society. As Alec said, you might look for and excuse such eccentricities in a lord's daughter, say, or a famous actor's; in an ex-insurance collector's it was really nothing but impudence. She had a cough, too, like a consumptive old man's. Alec was sure she'd die young.

No wonder Niven's subordinate whom Alec had once met by chance had called him an insincere bastard. That had been coarse pub talk, but, as Alec had said, trust a man's underlings to tell the truth about him. "You know, Nan, I wouldn't be surprised if big Niven landed up in jail. He's the kind it happens to. Sooner or later you'll hear of him trying to abscond with his firm's money."

And there was something else, which she had been so far too modest to mention to Alec: this was the greedy desperate look she now and then caught in Niven's eyes. Tonight it had been particularly noticeable. Judging by the Sunday newspapers, wasn't it very often his sort, the well-meaning ones by their way of it, the praisers of snow on trees, that in the end were arrested for indecency, as often as not with their own daughters?

3

BECAUSE HIS HAND was cold or nervous or guilty he had difficulty in putting the key in the Yale lock. Suddenly he was reminded again of the lorry's rattling arrival in the small town, the clatter of the rifles, and the quiet frightened hospitality offered by the two women, the one about his own age, the other white-haired. He heard again the roar of laughter, surprised and obsequious, when he, big Mungo, their strict fair-minded sergeant, had smashed the photograph of the grandson in the German officer's uniform, and then taken part in the looting. Of his share only the small silver eagle with outspread wings remained. He had told his family he had found it. "Helped yourself to it, you mean," Bess had said, indulgent to her victorious soldier. Andrew and Billy in turn, as small boys, had been disappointed because he had refused to support their big-eyed boasts that he must have got it from a dead German whom he had killed. For fifteen years he had put off telling them the truth. Perhaps tonight was the chance he had been waiting for.

In the small hallway, as he took off his hat and coat, he looked about him at the pathetic evidences of Bess's unimaginative home-making: the red candles in their tin holders on the wall, the picture of red and white roses bought at the Barrows, the patched carpet, and the brass jug useless for anything but keeping Billy's marbles in.

"That you, Mungo?" she cried from the living-room.

"Aye." He smelled egg and sausage, baked in the oven, one of his favourite dishes. She would have spent time and care seeing it was just as he liked it. Aye, but she never read a book from one year's end to the other, and did her best to keep him from reading any.

As he stood there he wondered if after all he would be able to tell her he was going to leave her. Not the dregs of his love for her, not loyalty to his children, not even a sense of right and wrong, would prevent him. No, he might be held captive until death by the innumerable coils of sheer commonplace habit.

The sitting-room door opened and Andrew, as tall as his father, came out, big-toothed with that insincerity of welcome he was not astute enough to dissemble or honest enough to dispense with. He had a book, open, in his left hand. It was Shakespeare's *Othello*.

"I say, Dad," he whispered, "could you possibly slip me half a crown or better still five bob? There's a meeting of the Mermaid Club at the Varsity tonight, and I'm skint. You wouldn't want me not to be able to pay for my tea and chocolate biscuits. I'm reading the part of Cassio."

"Haven't you asked your mother?"

"She's skint too, she says."

"And she says truly, you big moocher." Bess had come padding out in her torn slippers and old red cardigan, with bread-knife in hand. She smiled fondly at them both.

Mungo saw how whiter her hair was than he had realised, and also how, in this household which he intended to desert, she was the central prop. Perhaps it was the snow falling on those trees in the country that put the idea of lonely whiteness in his mind as he stared at her. Even as his heart yearned he saw how justified he would be in leaving her: how thick her legs, flabby her breasts, huge her belly, sloven her clothes, stupid her face, and everyday her soul. This fat woman with the untidy whitening hair was a stranger; worse, she was an enemy, winter, and never spring.

"It's a cauld night," she said. "You're shivering, Mungo.

Better go in to the fire. Pay no heed to this big scrounger." She winked at the scrounger as she said it. "I've got toast under the grill. Tell Peggy and Billy tea's ready. Get him to wash his hands."

"How is Peggy?" he asked. He could have addressed her on no other subject. "What did old Yellowlees say?"

Bess laughed. "He said she had a bad cough."

"We knew that, surely."

"Aye, but it was still a triumph of diagnosis for the auld man. He gave her a bottle. But I can smell that toast burning."

Laughing, she shuffled away. As he waited, as if for the murdering gun to be fired, the loose floorboard at the living-room doorway creaked sharply under her weight.

"Know this?" whispered Andrew. "It's not Peggy we should be worrying about. It's Mum."

Mungo was startled. "Your mother's never had a day's illness that I can mind of."

Andrew, rather facetiously, pressed his stomach. "She keeps getting a pain."

Mungo scowled. No doubt she did. It would be wind, and would be got rid of, without ceremony, when she was alone or in his company.

"She gobbles her food," he muttered.

"So she said herself. Anyway, it's not keeping her from the whist. She was saying she'd have to get the old snow-shoes oiled."

Mungo handed him two half crowns. "You're sure it's your club you're going to?"

"Where else, Dad?"

Mungo shrugged. If the lad wanted to sneak off to his Catholic shop-girl with the yellow hair and big breasts let him.

"Thanks a lot, Dad. Do you want an I.O.U. or is my word

good enough? You know I mean to pay back every penny."

"Who asked you to?"

"That's why I'm all the more determined to do it."

"We'll see."

They smiled at each other. Mungo's smile meant: "You don't intend to pay back a single ha'penny." And Andrew's meant: "To hell with the lot of you. I'll go to Ishbel if I want."

They slapped each other on the shoulder. Then Andrew went into the living-room to his mother, and Mungo into the sitting-room where he found Peggy and Billy seated at the table doing homework.

Mungo went over and turned the gas-fire on full. "It's cold in here," he said. "Well, thanks for rushing to welcome me."

"We're busy, Dad," said Billy, impatiently.

"So I see. Well, tea's ready. Off you go and wash your hands."

Billy rushed off gladly.

"Well, Peg, what about that cough? What did old Yellowlees say?"

She never hesitated about meeting his gaze; often it was he who had to look away. Without saying a word she seemed always to be setting him a test he could never hope to pass. Sometimes the reasons for his failure were obscure and he longed to ask her what they were; but most often they were plain enough.

As a small earnest chubby-cheeked child she had worshipped him, following him about, showing him her treasures, and using him as her standard by which to judge everyone else. Gradually she had changed. "Don't take it too much to heart, Mungo," Bess had said. "These things happen wi' lassies. She still thinks as highly of you, but it's mair complicated now. You see, she's discovered you're not perfect. But you're still her idol, though she'll not admit it."

26

"It's just an irritation," she replied. "It'll go away. He gave me a bottle."

"You'll have to take care, especially in weather like this."

Never had her grey eyes been so testing. "Dad."

"Yes?" He tried not to flinch.

"I've asked you this before. You said no."

"Well, ask again."

She did not trifle with any of the geometry instruments on the table. Long, thin, calm, her hands just lay. They reminded him, with a shudder, of Myra's.

"Can Robert Logan come here to stay with us for a day or two?"

So her paragon, her flower of chivalry, had been flung out of the house again by his drunken, self-pitying war-cripple of a father.

"Don't tell me the Logans have been at it again."

She let his own shame devour him. Then she said, "Robert's my friend."

He knew he should have laughed and said Logan was welcome. After all he himself would be gone tomorrow. But somehow he could not say it: he was not sure why.

"He could sleep on the floor, in here." She spoke quietly, as if this problem was as free from moral considerations as the geometry deduction she had been working out.

"Isn't he staying with old Mrs. Ralston? Isn't that his usual refuge?"

"Yes. But she's old, and a wee bit difficult. She keeps turning over the pages of his book. So it's hard to study."

"I thought he did all his studying in the public library."

"Can he come here?"

At her mercy, deserving no pity, he stumbled as so often before into hypocrisy. "There's your mother to consider, Peggy. Doesn't she complain as it is that we all give her too

27

much work to do? Andrew was telling me, too, she's not feeling very well."

"I help. Robert would give no trouble. He'd help too."

"Did you ask your mother?"

"Yes."

"What did she say?"

"It was your name on the door."

It was a favourite saying of Bess's. Well, after tonight that name plate would have to be taken down.

There was a banging on the door. Billy looked in. "Last call for tea. Mum says to tell you it's on the table getting cold." Then he raced off again.

"Please yourself," said Mungo. "I must say, though, I've never quite trusted young Logan."

She said nothing.

"I'm afraid you'll find out I'm right, Peggy."

She smiled faintly.

He tried to keep eagerness out of his voice. "What was Andrew talking about, when he said your mother isn't feeling well?"

"She gets a pain."

"That's common knowledge. She doesn't keep things like that a secret."

"I think this is different."

"In what way different?"

"More serious."

Was this a plot to keep him in his prison? "Why haven't I been told?"

"Mum said not to worry you."

"Why didn't she go with you to see old Yellowlees? Ah, I forgot: she's afraid of doctors."

"She's afraid of dying. We'd better go."

"Aren't we all?" he muttered.

But Bess's fear was pathological. Several times she had

28

woken up drenched in sweat from a nightmare of her own death. He had wondered why it had not kept her thin.

Certainly she was very subdued when he went into the living-room where they ate. Her face was grey. Perhaps, like an animal, she felt in her marrow a premonition. Hope turned him into her murderer.

"I suppose it's too late for grace," he said.

"It should never be too late for that, Mungo. Billy, Andrew, stop chewing."

Mungo kept his own eyes open, fixed on Peggy. The grace was one he had used at their Christmas dinner.

"Lord," he said, "as we thank you for this food, make us mindful of the millions of our fellow creatures throughout the world stricken with hunger at this very moment. Amen."

"Knox'll still not eat," said Billy. "He's getting awfully thin."

"I owe the auld chap an apology," said Bess. "I used to think cats never cared as long as their saucers were kept full. But Bridget Quinn specially bought some liver for him and he wouldn't lip it, not even when we rubbed it against his whiskers."

"Are you sure it was grief took away his appetite?" asked Mungo. "Maybe it was instinct warning him it was Catholic liver, liable to poison any cat that's been brought up a staunch Orangeman."

Andrew scowled.

Peggy's smile was too subtle for a peacemaker's. "I was reading that when the news of King Billy's victory at the Boyne reached Rome all the candles in the Vatican were lit in celebration."

Her mother seemed to have difficulty in concentrating. "True enough," she mumbled, "things were never as you imagined them."

"And why was His Holiness so pleased?" asked Mungo.

29

"He happened to be angrier at the time with Louis XIV of France than he was with the Protestants. So he preferred to see it as a slap in the face for Louis."

Her mother laughed. "Gie it ony name you like," she said, "religion or politics or war; go back as far as the Garden of Eden; and you find it's just human nature after all."

"And what else did you think it might be?" sneered Mungo.

"But it's so common, Mungo. Everybody's got it, rich and poor, high and low, fat and thin, sick and well. We're surrounded by it, all our lives. Human nature's just the folk we know. It's Wee Sprint Dougan, for example."

What respecter of intelligence, listening to such banalities, not to say idiocies, could blame him for having decided he had had enough? Yet he knew the answer he would have got from that old man in the bus. "She's your wife, isn't she? Did you marry her for her brains?"

The others were chatting merrily about Dougan, that veteran ex-bookie. Too old now to make intrepid escapes through closes and over wash-houses, he kept a betting-shop and wore big spotted bow-ties.

"And it's Mr. Duthie," said Billy.

Duthie was the grocer for whom Ishbel McKenzie worked. He pelted stray dogs with figs.

"And it's Belter McNaught," said Andrew, in revenge.

Billy frowned. McNaught was a teacher he feared.

"That's not fair," said Peggy.

Andrew sneered. "Who do you nominate, Peggy? Don't give us Robert Logan, for heaven's sake. It's human nature we're talking about, much too common for him, though he does have patches in the backside of his trousers."

"I would nominate Mrs. Ralston," said Peggy.

"Because she's taken in your hero again?"

"But she's daft," said Billy. "I mean, women with prams

rush away when they see her coming. She lifts the baby out whether she knows it or not."

"They say she was as hard in the head as the rest of us before her own twa weans died," said Bess. "She's had a sore life, twa weans and a man deid."

Mungo tried to see Bess as the corpse of the woman he had murdered by his hope, but he could not. Despite her unease, she kept smiling at him with affection, and rubbing her left breast.

Trembling, he decided that as a preparation to telling them he was leaving he would at last say how the silver eagle had descended out of a sky of horror into their home.

"I suppose," he began, "any man with imagination can feel he was present at all the great events in history."

"Such as old Jim Gallie's funeral?" suggested Bess.

The others laughed.

Her purpose was of course to keep him safely at her own level.

"Remember, Mungo? All flowers by special request to be orange or yellow, to match the sashes? And what a stushie when they thought the man driving the hearse was a pape because his name was Murphy."

"You can't always tell a Catholic by his name," observed Billy.

"It's mair reliable to judge by his face, son," said his mother. "It's usually got the map of Ireland written all over it."

Andrew scowled.

"You seem to be harping on death tonight, Bess," said Mungo.

"Me, Mungo? Nothing's further frae my thoughts. You'll have me to put up wi' for a long time yet."

"Since we're all so merry then," he said, "I want to tell you about an event in history I was present at."

She laughed. "I can just picture you running roond the Vatican helping to light a' those candles."

"What are you talking about?"

Andrew jumped up. "Excuse me. I've got an engagement."

Peggy rose too. "I'm going out."

"Don't be rude," cried their mother, laughing. "Your faither was about to tell us about this event in history he was present at."

"If you mean the war, Dad," said Billy, rather grudgingly, "I'll listen."

"That's it," said his mother. "You two go through to the sitting-room and slaughter mair Germans. The rest of us will clear the table and do the dishes. Flo's coming for me at a quarter to, and you know how she hates to be kept waiting."

"So," said Mungo, "you're going to the whist, though the snow's lying in the streets?"

She stared strangely at him. "It's just once a week, Mungo. It's not the whist so much either, it's the company. Why don't you come?"

Yes, if she had had her will she would have turned him too into a dreary whist-lover, like McTaggart's boy friend, that sly weasel Peffermill.

She came and put her hand on his arm. "Is there onything the matter, Mungo? Onything personal, at your work?"

"You mean: not, for God's sake, your starving millions?"

She smiled fondly. "We're your starving millions, Mungo, me and the weans."

He could not bear to be in her company any longer. He went through to the sitting-room, to consider what he should say in his letter of farewell.

4

As soon as the door closed behind him Andrew put his fingers to his nose at it. Then, laughing like Iago, he hurried downstairs. At old Mrs. Gallie's door he paused, and said, as evilly as he could: "Narrow-minded old bitch. I hope you die."

Out in the slushy street he pulled his hood over his head, and forgetting for a minute or two his father, his mother, Mrs. Gallie, and all the rest, let melt in his mind like the large flakes on his face the prospect of seeing Ishbel soon, and making love on the hearth-rug with HOME in yellow letters in its centre, while on the wall the green and blue geese would be flying towards the Virgin whose face would have been turned modestly away.

Soon icy misgivings flooded his mind. None concerned his father: his only dependence on him was financial and would soon end. It was different with his mother whom he loved and on whom he had always relied. She had made it very clear she disapproved of Ishbel and would violently oppose his marrying her. It had therefore been his mother's fault in a way that several weeks ago he had let himself be seduced by Ishbel, without the safeguard of the contraceptive that he had been carrying in his wallet for months. Before letting him penetrate her, Ishbel had picked it up with the coal tongs and dropped it into the fire, where it had shrivelled and hissed like a living thing.

Afterwards he had been suspicious that she would never have been so willing if she had never done it before, or if her mother had not put her up to it as a way of entrapping him.

B

Her last sweetheart had been a Catholic like herself, called Duffy. But more perennial than that suspicion was his foreboding that educationally she was not worthy and might harm his career as a teacher. Tutored no doubt by her small, grey-haired, wily mother, she had been quick to point out that he himself often spoke in a slovenly local way. Yes, but this was to youths who had been at school with him and who nowadays hooted after him with more or less good-humoured derision. If not placated these might turn nasty some dark night.

Intellectually Ishbel was a dunce, far more interested in showing off a new dress or perfume than in reading a book or in listening to him read. After five minutes or less she would begin to fidget and yawn, and start persuading him how much pleasanter and more natural it would be for them to caress each other with the lights low and the television on.

Peggy said, ironically but truthfully, that once escape from the ghetto of social inferiority was determined on you had to be without scruple. In the war escapers had killed guards and left their comrades still in prison to suffer the reprisals. Andrew was well aware how very difficult, if not impossible, it would be to dig through the solid concrete of having for your wife someone out of whose mouth, however exquisitely lipsticked, issued crudities of mispronunciation fitter for a factory girl. Once safely out, too, you had to continue to be vigilant and remorseless if you wanted to stay out. Even if they had to be sent to a fee-paying school your children must be pertinaciously fashioned so as to consolidate your advance and carry it further. It was essential therefore that you provided them with a mother able to help nurture them towards that end.

Yet he loved Ishbel and would have gone through snow knee-deep, just for the joy of rubbing his cheek against her yellow hair. One marvellous consequence of her lack of

34

education was that she, and only she, admired him as in his heart he thought he deserved to be admired. Faults at which others, including his mother, laughed, were by her admiration turned to virtues. She thought brilliant his every platitude and plagiarism. Unsure of himself, and knowing how intellectually old-fashioned he really was compared with Peggy and Robert Logan, his pride had come to need her so ravenously that it could not bear to lose her, at any rate not at present. Always, however, in a part of his mind kept veiled, he was conscious that if ever he gained enough self-confidence not to need her red-lipped yellow-haired soft-bosomed flattery, then, if it was not too late, he would be able to find the callousness to forsake her and marry instead some teaching colleague. Two teachers' salaries would mean, very quickly, a bungalow and a car.

He must take care it was never too late.

As he trudged along he beat his fist against the book in his pocket. He wanted to start running to get to her, to tell her he loved her or to curse her for having ensnared him, to make love to her on the white rug or to suffocate her with one of the blue cushions. It was monstrously unfair that he should be placed in such a position. It was his father's fault. If he had been a doctor or a teacher or even a factory manager instead of an insurance collector who had left school at fourteen, then Andrew would not have been brought up in the same district as Ishbel, and he would never have met her.

Ishbel's mother, that small shrewd purse-clutcher, knew so much about his family's background it must have been the outcome of diligent ferreting. She had remarked, as if it was to everybody's credit, that his father had been brought up in Culdean Street, one of the city's toughest and meanest, by an old aunt who had kept a ragstore and had gone about the streets pushing a barrow and blowing a trumpet. Humiliated and out-manœuvred, Andrew had hurried home to ask his

35

mother if it was true. She had wanted to know who had told him, though it was evident she had already guessed. Never had he seen her so angry and contemptuous. "Three quarters of them are on public assistance, for all their holy water. They came across from Ireland with nothing but pigs' dirt sticking to their feet. And yet they have the impudence to spread slander about those who have seen through them." He hadn't dared to point out that Ishbel's forebears came from the Hebrides. When he had consulted Peggy she had reacted as he might have expected. "A trumpet? I heard it was a bugle. And she hadn't a barrow, she carried a bag on her back. And she wore a man's cap. I wish I could have met her."

As he waited, huddled in a butcher's shopdoor, wondering whether to dash across the puddled street or turn and slink away for good, he thought of his father with shiver after shiver of hate and sympathy.

That street where the McKenzies lived was in an area that dwellers in villas or bungalows with gardens would have called slumdom, but which, in the view of its inhabitants, was just saved from that disgrace by their own brave efforts to preserve respectability. It was so close to the gasworks, and so surrounded by factories, that tonight the slush in Andrew's chilled nostrils stank like Mrs. Gallie's carpets. Thick-walled and small-windowed, like civilian barracks, these tenements were well over a hundred years old. Dourly they awaited demolition, their stonework flaking and crumbling, their outside lavatories forever leaking and sighing. Behind were the backcourts where the earth looked, felt, smelled, and even tasted like dirt, as every child in its infancy discovered. In summer a few dandelions, known as pee-the-beds, boldly grew in corners, but were visited by no bees or butterflies. Occasionally a rat, bound for the garbage bins, sniffed at their gold.

The McKenzies' house, in one of those tenements, was clean and quite nicely furnished on the hire-purchase system. Mrs. McKenzie was known in the district as a good manager. She could make her man's wage as a brickie's labourer and her own as a scrubber of offices go a miraculously long way. Andrew had to respect her but he feared her too. Knowing that she herself would never get out of the ghetto, acknowledging indeed that her proper place was in it, she had devoted her whole life to preparing a way out for her daughter. She had therefore gratuitously vowed that when he and Ishbel got married, in a Catholic church of course, and went to live among their social equals, neither she nor her husband would ever cause them a minute's shame or inconvenience.

Andrew swore. He was a bloody fool to stand shivering there. There were plenty of places to go to: a cinema; back home even, where his father need not be heeded; the public library, where he could at least jeer at Robert Logan; or even the Varsity.

At last, angry with Ishbel for causing him all this perplexity, but more and more in need of the comfort she could give, he ran across the street through puddles golden in the lamplight. As he entered the close a small black dog came sneaking out. It had been sheltering without sanction and now fled, afraid of kicks and stones. He stared after it in horror and pity: in its small thin cowed hindquarters seemed to be concentrated all his own timidities and apprehensions.

Therefore when Ishbel opened the door and said huffily, "I was beginning to think you was never coming," he made for her like a murderer, clutched her, so warm and soft in her blue dress, in his cold wet arms, pressed her against the wall, and kissing her muttered, "Were, were, were," with as much passion as the Moor had cried, "Be sure thou provst my wife a whore."

He let her push him off at last.

"For heaven's sake, Andrew," she said, laughing. "Look, you're soaked. And you've got the wallpaper all wet. It's just as well my mother's not here to see it."

"It'll dry," he said, thinking that blood too would dry.

Tenderly she helped him off with his drenched coat. "You're privileged, you know. Dad's got to stand on sheets of newspaper, and take off all his working clothes, before being allowed into the living-room."

When she led him in by the hand he saw at once that the Virgin's face was already turned to the wall, and the geese therefore, flying towards her, seemed, like him, to have no purpose or destination.

5

FLORENCE MCTAGGART HAD been widowed by the war and left with two small sons to bring up. Showered with public praises of her husband's sacrifice, and then dismissed with a mean pension, she had come to see it as her duty to expose, wherever she detected it and often where her interference was not welcome, the gap between pretension and performance. She refused to make an iota of allowance for inevitable human shortcomings. By no mean exempt were her own two sons who, after being valiantly escorted across the desert of respectable poverty, had lost no time in repaying her with ingratitude and desertion. Dugald, the older, a carpenter, had married a hard-faced blonde ten years his senior, who had listened with fag in mouth to Flo's accusation that the pregnancy making the marriage necessary could not be Dugald's doing, and then had jerked her dagger-like thumb in the direction of the door, with two words only, one of them the vilest in the language. Flo had never spoken to her or Dugald since, nor had she seen the child, now a boy of three. Gilbert, her second son, had emigrated to Canada and sent her two letters in as many years.

Mungo had once said bitterly: "Sir Alexander Fleming noticed that certain kinds of staphlycocci were inhibited by the mould called penicillin. I've noticed that every kind of ideal or generous thought is inhibited by a woman called McTaggart."

Laughing, Bess had answered: "What you mean is, Mungo, wee Flo's hard on frauds."

That night in the taxi on the way to the whist Flo, neat in

ponyskin coat, wore also her sharpest face. As they passed Donnelly's Howff, the most popular pub in the district, they caught a glimpse over the frosted glass of men standing at the bar.

"Look at them," said Flo, "as conceited as kings."

But at that moment Bess was feeling the first really bad stound of pain since last night in bed beside Mungo. Those stabs at tea-time had been bearable enough. For her the men in the cosy pub, rattling the hard-earned silver in their pockets, and talking about football, racing, and women, represented not conceit at all but many other things necessary to make up a happy human life. She loved them all and was grateful to them, even to drunkards that gave their wives an odd skelp or two and wasted on booze what ought to have been spent on food and clothes for their families.

"They've worked hard all day, Flo. They're entitled to a bit of relaxation."

"I'd relax them. Whatever glory they think they've got I'd slice it off."

Bess tried to laugh.

"Don't laugh, Bess. Leniency's no virtue. It gets you nowhere. I'd have thought you for one would have learned that lesson."

It was another dig at Mungo. Previously Bess had been indulgent towards those digs as showing a kind of upside-down admiration, but tonight, desperate for Mungo's love and support, she must not let him be miscalled.

"What I've learned, Flo," she said, her hair damp with sweat, "is to be grateful when I'm judged wi' leniency. As, thank God, I always have been." Suddenly she was in tears.

Luckily Flo was staring out of the window. "Never be too humble," she muttered.

Even if it is cancer, Bess thought, as it was with Chrissie Peffermill, and I was dying in agony as she did, I still couldn't give Andrew my blessing to marry that McKenzie girl. I would never rest in my grave if my grandweans were being brought up to kiss beads and dab their brows with holy water.

"D'you think little Ebenezer will be there tonight?" she asked, merely to talk, to be friendly.

Flo decided that this reference to her suitor, by a name that he disliked, was in retaliation. Therefore she refused to heed it and stared all the harder out of the window.

So Bess was able to concentrate on trying to cajole the pain into a corner of her mind where it could be made to lie down and rest. It was a great help to think about Mungo. The greater the difference between what he really was and what he wanted to be, the fonder she felt and somehow the more dependent. That he was not contented must to some degree be her fault: she would have to try harder to humour him and stop teasing. Yet she could not help smiling as she pictured him, in monk's garb, running barefooted through the Vatican lighting all the candles.

"Burn it doon, while you're at it, Mungo," she murmured.

"What's that?" asked Flo sharply.

"Nothing, Flo. I was just talking to myself."

Before Flo could comment they arrived at the Masonic Hall. Old Tom Adams, the caretaker, greeted them.

"If it wasnae for you whist fiends," he grumbled, "I wouldn't hae needed to leave my fireside. I doot if an H-bomb would keep you lot away."

"Go down to Donnelly's and tell them that," retorted Flo.

In the whist room the players were huddled near the radiators. They greeted Bess and Flo, but Bess especially, with comradely cries. They had been discussing Bingo. This week still more of their company had deserted to that new craze.

"Did you ken, Bess," cried Jean Aird, wearing a hat like a

41

helmet, "they've even taken ower that old empty church in Willow Street."

"So I heard, Jean. And what does our elder, Mr. Peffermill, say to that?"

Mr. Peffermill preferred to say nothing. Small and dapper, he had a habit of shutting his eyes every so often, not in involuntary blinks like a smelter in the steelworks, but as deliberate withdrawals of the honour of his gaze and attention. His voice was so high he seemed always to be on his tiptoes when speaking, and he said nothing, not even the time of day, without solemnity. There were many who found it hard to stomach his prim, brisk self-importance. He was the first to reprove any user of profane or dirty talk, but he always managed to give Bess, and others too, the impression that in his house, in a drawer under his white shirts, would be found pictures of naked women. She was often tempted, when Flo criticised Mungo, to retaliate at wee Peffy's expense; but she mostly refrained, for after all he carried the plate on Sundays or welcomed worshippers at the kirk door, and in any case when all was said and done what harm was there in a man with a dead wife consoling himself with pictures of plump young whores?

As soon as he could Mr. Peffermill drew his Florence aside, a lady to her finger-tips, in comparison with this gross vulgar boor, Niven, whose laughter at her own crude jokes was only paralleled in its raucousness by the bellow of a female hippo in heat, and whose husband, a man seldom at church but a reader, it seemed, of *The Confessions of St. Augustine*, among other books, was rumoured to be seeking comfort and refuge with daintier women.

"Florence, my pet," he whispered, "you know I am still waiting for you to name the happy date."

She glanced round to see if any had heard him. They were all too busy laughing at Bess, or waiting to be made laugh.

42

"Soon, my dear," he urged. "Please make it soon."

She smiled and nodded. She had always thought he should have been a man of the cloth; and it had been her ambition, as a girl at Sunday school, to be lady of the manse some day.

Was it, Mr. Peffermill wondered, St. Augustine who had written, after a licentious youth, that the only purpose of copulation was to procreate?

At his age, and Florence's, they certainly did not want children; but each would want the full and delicious benefit of the other's body. Just as fat women, like Niven, turned out to be light-footed dancers, so small lady-like ones, in public so discreet, in bed proved adepts at married venery.

When play began Bess, for the moment not in pain, found her luck remarkable. Being one whom the simplest of surprises pleased, the delight of picking up her cards one by one was seldom spoiled, even if they turned out to be mostly rags. Tonight, though, for those first nine wonderful hands she saw only aces, face cards, and trumps. It was as if she was being compensated for the agony in the taxi. Not to God, but to Mungo was the credit. Therefore every trick she won was for him. It was childish to think so, but she liked to be childish in this way. Her laughter brought smiles and well-disposed remarks even from those whose luck was out. It was like having a fire to sit at, on a snowy night, just listening to Bess Niven laugh. At two tables Mungo was mentioned, with censure: You'd think a man with such a cheery and popular wife would be willing to be seen in her company once in a while. But no, there were folk who thought she was a widow, like McTaggart.

By a coincidence, when the pain struck again, worse than ever, during the dealing of the tenth hand, Flo was her woman opponent, with Bod Aird as partner, that slow-witted friendly big man who had a habit of humming Scots songs as

43

he cogitated. People complained that he thus revealed his hands. If he had a good one he would hum 'O open the door some pity to show' or some other such mournful tune; but if he had a poor one he would choose a jaunty tune, like 'I'll aye ca' in by yon toon.' Even those who complained had to smile and forgive. His wife Jean was as burly as he, and perhaps to suit the increasing hairiness of her chin wore hats of aggressive shapes.

Bess's own partner was Mr. Peffermill.

Just as she reached out to pick up her third card, the three of diamonds it was, the pain struck. The room spun, all her blood and with it her life, seemed to pour out of her like a waterfall. She gasped.

"What's the matter?" asked Flo.

"Nothing. My old trouble. Indigestion. Hope the gentlemen don't mind me mentioning it. My own gentleman says I eat my food too fast."

"We all do," observed Mr. Peffermill. "According to the experts we ought to devote at least forty chews to every mouthful. No one has the patience. It also depends of course on the efficiency of one's teeth."

He spoke slowly, to accommodate his partner whose hands, usually so dexterous, kept fumbling. Already she had dropped two of her cards, letting their opponents see them. Her knee bumped against the leg of the table and sent Aird's ash-tray dancing. Sweat appeared on her brow as magically as dew. She was of course much too stout to be healthy. As diagnostician, not as lecher, he imagined her unclothed: those huge breasts like lumps of lard gone bad in the centre, that great swollen tun of a belly, those massive thighs, and the neck that would turn any double string of pearls into a single, all these must put a great strain on the heart. He would not be surprised really if she were to drop down dead with the next card she played. Diagnosis over, he reneged for a moment and considered her as a partner in what Burns had called houghmagandy. The result was some grudging sympathy for her husband, despite the latter's intellectual pretensions. Mr. Peffermill did not quite believe Niven had ever read *St. Augustine's Confessions*. A man with such a wife just could not read such books.

She saw his small pale smirking face across a great green prairie. She thought she must be dead, and he was the first to greet her. She wondered why he looked so heartless. Why, too, was she still suffering? And where was her mother?

"Bess, we're waiting," said Flo.

"I have," said Aird, with heavy tact, "a Rennie or two, if you'd care for them." Pulling up his thick grey pullover, he searched through his waistcoat pockets.

"No thanks," she muttered, still in a daze.

He pushed across two tablets. "They look a bit stoury, Bess. But they'll be clean enough when you take the wrappers off. It's a mistake to go on suffering considering that relief is so simple."

"Sometimes not so simple," said Mr. Peffermill. "Our intestines lie coiled within us like sluggish pythons."

"No talking," said Flo.

Aird smiled at Bess, who was sucking his tablets. He was glad he had been able to help.

Mr. Peffermill imagined the trickle of alkalined saliva creeping down to try and appease the great snake.

Bess was sure she would never rise from that table alive. Under her breath she kept repeating her children's names and her husband's.

"You've got a club surely?" demanded Flo.

She looked; she had two. "Sorry, Flo."

"It's not like you to let your mind wander."

"She needs her tea," said Aird.

Mr. Peffermill mused on. Surely it could not be plain

indigestion that was causing his expert partner to renege, sweat, fumble, and worst of all look so grotesquely lovelorn? Might it not be something akin to what had killed his own Chrissie, a malady of those mysterious organs woman had in them, wombs shaped like Drambuie bottles, ovaries, Fallopian tubes, and little glands with curious functions? Chrissie had been operated on twice. Emaciated, with skin like scorched paper, she had given the knife no trouble. Fat Bess on the other hand would need an excavation; he felt his wrist ache in sympathy with the surgeon's. These were ungentlemanly thoughts; but oh Beelzebub, how stupidly, how unconscientiously, the woman was playing.

At the finish, having helped to lose every trick but two, Bess apologised, spoiling it with characteristic facetiousness; she knew very well how he disliked being addressed as Ebenezer. In revenge he noted that she was still in pain. No need for him to rebuke her; she was in just hands; as indeed were they all.

She rose, almost knocking the table over. "Sorry," she gasped. "Excuse me. Back in a minute. Come with me, Flo."

"It's the interval anyway," said Flo, "and not our turn with the tea." She excused herself like a lady.

Aird grinned as he lit a fag and looked after them. "Wind's the devil if you don't get rid of it."

Mr. Peffermill frowned.

"Funny how women always like company to go to these places," went on the big engine-driver. "Don't tell me it's just to save a penny. It's an instinct they have, to gang up against us. We cause the wars that kill their bairns, you see. We're the flies in the ointment, you might say."

Mr. Peffermill did not care to be dragged down to this level. "I do not think women should be joked about."

Aird nodded, remembering that his companion's wife had

46

died in agony not much more than a year ago. "Still, they joke plenty about us; big Bess especially."

"They are the sources of life."

Nodding again at what seemed at first far profounder than his own fireside commonplaces, Aird looked round at all those sources of life, his own Jean prominent among them, wearing a white stiff furry hat, and munching her jaws. Few of the others seemed to him any bonnier: each had her own peculiarities, which he was too magnanimous to enumerate. Earlier he had been at a table where there had been whispers about Mungo Niven and some young woman called Fraser. He had said nothing but in his heart had sided with Bess. Granted she carried more fat than was comely or necessary, but it scarcely deserved betrayal, especially when it had been accumulated, you might say, in her man's daily sight, at his table, in his bed, with his money, and bearing his children. Now though, with wee Peffermill sneering in so superior a way, he wasn't so sure. All very well to call them the sources of life and honour them as such, but Peffermill had never had any children of his own and, so it was said, had small patience with other folks'. It seemed inconsistent to honour the sources of life and then condemn life itself, on its two legs, as damned noisy nuisances.

6

THE MOMENT SHE swung open the door and saw Robert in his usual corner in front of the reference books that nobody but himself ever seemed to refer to, Peggy forgot her soaked feet, her shivers, her coughing, and even, more intimate and distressing than all those, her father's desperate hypocrisy. Crossing the large silent room she took care not to show her joy.

Miss Bryce, the strictest attendant, was on duty at the desk. She was about forty, quite good-looking, with a big bosom and reddish hair. Her mouth drooped and her greeny-grey eyes sulked, in an unhappiness resentful and curiously public. Her colleagues ignored some of the out-of-date regulations, but she applied them all as if they were a code of revenge. There was a rule against eating in the Reading Room. Therefore if she saw so much as an apple being surreptitiously munched or a peppermint sucked she would come stalking out of her enclosure and forbid it. That there should be silence was sensible enough, but occasions could arise surely, especially with most of her patrons so old, when there might be, for instance, the news of a death to communicate. She would not allow even that. The private pechings, gruntings, sighings, sniggerings, and weepings of the solitary old men would be rebuked too, hardly because they were disturbing to others but because they were the utterances of loneliness. For she was the loneliest of all.

Often there was a hunger in her eyes. Robert had been displeased with Peggy for suggesting it was sexual.

"All you disciples of Freud," he had said. "You can only think of the one thing."

Tonight, to Peggy's surprise, as she passed the desk Miss Bryce called her back. "Miss Niven!"

Peggy had not known the woman knew her name. She prepared for a lecture about coming in looking and barking like a drenched dog.

But Miss Bryce was nervously smiling. "Please remember this is a Reading Room," she said, "where people come to read. Those who want to chat should go to a café."

Peggy could not help looking round. The old men scattered about the room wouldn't have minded had she burst out singing. Two were asleep. One, fifty years away, was moving his teeth in his mouth. Another was reading with a magnifying glass. Still another was poking his pinkie into his ear and turning it slowly round like a corkscrew.

All the same, she had been annoyed herself once or twice by young toughs who had come in for a carry-on.

"All right," she said.

"Your friend's been engrossed for the past two hours."

Peggy saw with amazement that she was blushing.

One of the old men, thinking that if the guardian of silence could break it herself, so might he, looked up from the newspaper he was reading, and called out, in hoarse incredulity, to a crony yards away. "D'you see this, Wullie? The Turks still owe us eight hundred thoosand pounds for the Crimean War."

Miss Bryce rapped on the desk with a pencil. "Silence, please," she cried, but not so peevishly as usual.

"I understand," she whispered, "his father is a war-cripple."

She was blushing again.

What's this, wondered Peggy. Part of it anyway was impertinent curiosity which had to be dourly discouraged. She frowned and said nothing.

"And they live in a room and kitchen."

49

Peggy went on frowning.

"With six of them in the family." Miss Bryce paused. "You may think these questions inquisitive, Miss Niven."

Peggy gave one dour nod.

"I have reasons for asking them. You see, I can't regard him as a stranger. For months now I've watched him sit over there and study, so steadfastly. I've often thought he deserved help."

"Has he ever asked for it?"

"No. I don't think he would ever do that."

Peggy wasn't so sure. She liked Robert but didn't quite understand him.

"He has a large bruise on his face," whispered Miss Bryce, with astonishing anger. "I believe it was his father who did it, in drunken rage. That shouldn't be allowed."

"They love each other." Unlike her own father and Andrew, between whom existed a peace of indifference.

"Love!" Miss Bryce was horrified. "I think it's dreadful, so devoted a student not getting a decent chance. We should all be ashamed of ourselves."

One of the old men daringly said, "Wheehst!"

Peggy smiled, but Miss Bryce looked furious.

"Sarcastic old fool," she muttered.

Peggy walked across to where Robert sat scribbling ecstatically one moment and the next staring up at the ceiling as if seraphim were painted there, blowing trumpets.

"Hello, Peggy," he said, with a grin. "Was she giving you a telling-off?"

Peggy sat beside him, close enough to be compassionately aware he hadn't had a bath for some time. The snobbish and fastidious Miss Bryce too would have noticed that. There was a purplish bruise on his left cheek, and over all his face, in spite of its brown-eyed, long-lipped sensitiveness, were the more familiar marks of his having had all his eighteen years to eat cheap food, wear shoddy clothes, and sleep in a room with three or four others.

To her annoyance she could not speak for coughing.

"You shouldn't have come, Peggy. You're soaked to the skin."

"So are you."

"I've not got a cough. Did you go to the doctor?"

"Yes. He gave me a bottle."

"Make sure you take it then."

"Is your face sore?"

"No."

Miss Bryce was staring over at them.

"I spoke to my father," whispered Peggy.

Robert stared at the pencil in his hand, and smiled. "You shouldn't have, Peggy. I asked you not to."

"Well, I did. And he said all right."

"Are you sure?"

"Of course. Why shouldn't I be?"

"I've got a feeling your father doesn't like me, Peggy." He smiled. "I think he's jealous. And he doesn't think I'm good enough for you."

"Why are you talking such rubbish?"

"I'm all right with old Maggie, you know."

"She pesters you with silly kindnesses. You've said so." She did not want yet to bring up the subject of Miss Bryce's blushing interest in him. "What's going to be done about all this, anyway? Because he's your father doesn't give him a right to hit you, especially when he knows you won't hit him back."

"You know it isn't just so simple as that, Peggy."

No, it wasn't. Sober, Mr. Logan was sensitive and intelligent; drunk, he was violent with self-pity and revengefulness. "They're so bloody anxious about making the Germans whole again. Who's interested in making me whole?" She

51

knew, too, how he had been made to feel ashamed at having begot children. This was thought by his neighbours to be scandalous, not just because the State would have to pay for their upbringing, but also because, in puritanic and prurient imaginations, those crippled begettings were seen as revolting. She had overheard Mrs. McTaggart say: "Only a woman without a scrap of pride would have agreed to it. Don't tell me it was love."

She caught sight of Miss Bryce staring over at them. "There's another one that's jealous."

"Who?"

"Sexy Maud."

He frowned. She remembered what Billy said about him, that his hands were too small. So they were, small and somehow not altogether trustworthy. Immediately she felt ashamed of herself.

"Forget it," she said. "I'm sorry."

But he would not forget it; he was too interested. "What did she say?"

"She was asking all sorts of questions about you. She said you deserve help."

"What kind of help?"

"That's what I wondered."

Suddenly Miss Bryce shouted, "Time, please." Her voice was hoarse.

The old men stirred, woke one another up, took last anxious glances at newspapers or magazines, peered up at the clock, were dismayed to find they were being cheated out of two and a half minutes, shuddered at the prospect of icy slippery streets and inhospitable firesides, rose with creaking and aching bones, mumbled "Guid-night" to Miss Bryce, as if appealing to her, and went out.

Robert gathered up his papers and books and pushed them into his khaki knapsack.

"If she speaks to us," said Peggy, "just say good-night and that's all."

He grinned. "You certainly don't like her, Peggy."

"I don't trust her."

"Do you mean she pockets the fines for keeping books out too long?"

Peggy realised she did not quite know what she meant. "I just don't trust her."

"An intellectual depending on instinct? I'm surprised at you, Peggy."

Miss Bryce stopped them at her desk. "I've had my eye on you two," she said, archly. She did not sound like herself.

"I ought to apologise," said Robert. "I know we blether too much."

Miss Bryce simpered. "Gracious me, I was just joking."

"No. Silence is a sensible rule in a Reading Room."

Peggy noticed he was blushing. So too was Miss Bryce.

"Let's go, Robert," she said. "Good-night."

They ignored her.

"Has your friend told you how much I've admired the way you study so indomitably?" asked the librarian.

"Peggy did say something. Nothing indomitable about it, I'm afraid. It's just got to be done."

"My brother, you know, was killed in the war. He was in the R.A.F. He was hardly any older than you."

"I'm sorry."

"Oh, I'm afraid I've almost forgotten him now. My mother hasn't, though. She still grieves for him. She still hoards his clothes."

Is that all it is, thought Peggy: she's trying to find some reasonably gracious way of offering him her brother's clothes. But if so, why these smiles, creating an intimacy from which she herself was being shut out?

Oh, for heaven's sake, she told herself, don't be any viler

53

than you can help. A woman whom you thought aloof and snobbish is showing herself interested; a boy who needs help badly sees a chance of getting some. That she was almost old enough to be his mother made it all the more respectable, rather than otherwise.

Yes, but Miss Bryce kept looking like a woman with more to offer than cast-off clothes, and Robert like a boy too eager to find out what it was.

"I understand you're in trouble at home," said Miss Bryce, her voice deep with sympathy.

"It's nothing, really."

"A matter of accommodation, I suppose. It's quite absurdly unfair. There you are three or four to a room, and my mother and I share a house with four bedrooms."

"He's coming to stay with us for a day or two," said Peggy.

He shook his head. "I couldn't do that, Peggy. It's very kind of you, but you really haven't got room."

"Well, at old Maggie Ralston's you've got a room to yourself."

"Yes, but you know Maggie."

"Is she the old woman who comes in and looks at the fashion magazines?" asked Miss Bryce. "Dressed like a tramp? With an unfortunate habit of spitting on the floor?"

"There's nobody kinder," said Peggy dourly. "And with her kindness is for kindness' sake."

The insinuation was disregarded.

"I'm sure her house can't be clean," said Miss Bryce.

"She means well," said Robert ruefully, "but she can be such an old nuisance. I mean, she waits beside me to turn over the pages when I'm reading."

"You used to find that funny and touching," snapped Peggy.

"I still do, but it can be annoying."

54

"I should think so," said Miss Bryce. "Well, would you like to accept my mother's offer? Because it is hers. I've told her all about you. She'd be delighted to have you."

Robert laughed. "This is tremendously kind of you, Miss Bryce, and of your mother."

"You would be the one showing kindness. As I've said, my mother still misses my brother."

"When?" He hesitated, smiling.

"Tonight. Why not? What would be the point in waiting?"

"But your mother can't be expecting me."

"I'll give her a ring and prepare her."

Then they were interrupted by her two colleagues from the Lending Department. They had on their outdoor clothes and looked displeased to see her wasting time chatting.

"About ready, Maud?" asked one.

"Oh, Ethel, I'm sorry I'm going to be a little delayed. Will you and Molly just go on without me?"

They looked still more displeased. Peggy and Robert got scowls.

"It's such a filthy night," they said. "The snow's lying."

"I'm sorry. I'll lock up."

"Very well. It's your car, but you might at least have given us some notice."

"There's a bus-stop fifty yards away."

They went off angrily, with last glowers at Peggy and Robert.

"I hope we haven't interfered with your usual arrangements?" said Robert.

"Not at all. I usually run them home in my car. It doesn't do to make moral obligations out of such favours. Well, I'll go and let Mother know we're coming, shall I?"

Off she went, without waiting for a reply.

With so much to say and so little time, Peggy had just then to be seized with a bad fit of coughing. It reverberated

55

through the large silent room. Trying hard to control it brought tears of annoyance to her eyes.

Robert was sympathetic but it was really Miss Bryce's astonishing offer his mind was on.

"Stupid," Peggy managed to say at last. "How stupid can you be?"

"What do you mean?"

"Aren't small boys warned not to accept gifts from strange women in public parks?"

He put on his haughtiest look. "What on earth are you havering about?"

"You know all right."

"If I knew I wouldn't have asked, would I?"

"Don't you think it's extraordinary, after seeing you for months and hardly so much as looking at you, she should suddenly take it into her head to invite you to her house?"

"Of course it's extraordinary." His voice had gone shrill. "The Good Samaritan was extraordinary, wasn't he?"

Before Peggy could find an answer to that Miss Bryce came hurrying back, dressed in her outdoor clothes and clapping her gloved hands in front of her like a Salvation Army girl with cymbals.

"What did I tell you?" she cried. "My mother's simply delighted. She's expecting us in half an hour."

Peggy turned to him. "Won't Maggie be expecting you too?"

"That's no difficulty," said Miss Bryce. "We'll call in on her on our way. I have a car. What about you, Miss Niven? Can we offer you a lift?"

"No thanks. I'll walk."

"But, Peggy," said Robert, "you shouldn't, you know. That's a bad cough you've got."

"It is," agreed Miss Bryce.

"You look after yourself," Peggy said to him, unable to keep the—jealousy, was it?—out of her voice.

56

As she waited outside on the pavement while Miss Bryce with Robert's help locked the door, and as she followed them round the corner to where the yellow Anglia was parked, furred with snow, she kept telling herself she was a dirty-minded bitch, and there was nothing evil or nightmarish about the situation at all. On the contrary, the icy desolateness of the streets emphasised the need for loving-kindness, such as Miss Bryce, and her mother, were showing. The mistake ought never to be made that only people one liked were good, just as it should never be assumed that those one disliked were always wrong.

I suppose, she thought, there really is a Mrs. Bryce.

Robert again urged her to accept a lift. Again she refused.

From inside the car Miss Bryce said: "Why not come and visit Robert at the week-end?"

"I'll see him at school tomorrow."

"So you will. But that needn't prevent you from visiting him at the week-end."

"What about your mother?" Peggy asked him. "And your father?"

"I intend to see Robert's parents myself," said Miss Bryce. "But tomorrow will do. Good-night, Miss Niven. I'm sorry we can't help you."

"I don't need help."

"Good-night, Peggy," he said. "Go straight home."

As she watched the car drive away she tried, as always, to console herself by thinking about her family: her mother presiding over the whist, as over everything, with laughter and goodwill; Andrew, by the McKenzie fireside, happy and proud, though Ishbel had as usual preferred watching television to listening to him read; and Billy in bed, safe and warm, innocent even in his dreams.

She did not include her father.

7

MUNGO KEPT TELLING himself everything was for the last time: filling the hot water bottles and putting them in the beds; inspecting Billy's neck and ears after the hasty wash; buttering the cream crackers and heating the milk for cocoa for his son's supper; watching Billy, shiny-faced, eat and drink while looking at a comic; and then, with finger on light switch, saying good-night. All these things, usually done by Bess, but by him often enough, would after tonight never be done by him again. Therefore about every simple familiar act was a sense of finality, of loss, and of personal inadequacy, as poignant as in the presence of death.

It was amazing that Billy noticed nothing different and chatted about football, Knox the cat, marbles, and school, more eagerly indeed than he did with his mother; the excess, alas, not springing from superior love.

About to put out the light Mungo sighed loudly. "At a football match," he said, "you'll have noticed how it's always more exciting if you're supporting one of the teams?"

"Sure, Dad. Me for the 'Gers every time."

Mungo decided not this time to rebuke his son for siding with the successful and powerful. "Sometimes, though," he added, "in life, in more important things than football, it's wise not to take sides."

Billy yawned. "You mean, between the Americans and the Russians?"

"I mean something more important than that even."

He switched out the light.

Billy waited: his lack of interest, and the cat-like

cautiousness of his affection, could be felt in the dark.

What could Myra ever have to do with all this? Or Barcelona with its sunny plazas and its monument of Columbus?

"Between a boy's father and mother, it could be." It was out, in spite of the lump of shame in his throat. "Whatever has happened in the past, whatever may happen in the future, don't you take sides. Wait till you're of an age to understand. We both love you. I know you've always seemed more attached to your mother; that's natural."

The lump grew too big.

Billy was silent. Then he murmured, guilefully, "Dad, is it true what Peggy said? That Robert Logan's coming here to stay with us? I hope it isn't. Andrew and me don't like him much. He's got such wee hands." He laughed, but was in earnest.

Mungo was not concerned for Robert Logan. "Don't harden your heart, Billy," he said, with passion. "Have pity. If you can't afford it at your age when can you? All over the world, in this very street where we live, in this house, God knows, people are unhappy, in doubt, crucified almost, deserving of pity at least."

"Peggy said you said he could come. Did you, Dad?"

Baffled, Mungo could find nothing more to say.

"But you don't like him, Dad. You said so."

"Did I? I had no right to judge the boy."

"It would be horrible if he was here. You've got to say no, Dad. If you leave it to Mum she'll say yes, as sure as eggs. She's too soft."

"You think so?" Within, he cried: Your mother in her own way is as ruthless as that monster with female breasts who at Buchenwald had a lampshade made out of human skin. She has made a joke, a toy, of my very soul.

"Sure. Look how she always believes Andrew."

"You mean, he wasn't going to this Mermaid Club of his?"

59

Billy did not answer. He had already said too much: he had betrayed his fellow conspirator. He muttered, "Goodnight, Dad. I'll need to get to sleep. We're getting an algebra test tomorrow."

Mungo sneered. Surrounded by lies, guile, and distrust, why should he feel any contrition at all? "I notice you never say your prayers now."

"Just sometimes. I don't kneel on the floor, though. It's too hard. I say them in bed. It's just as good, isn't it?"

"And will you say them tonight after I've gone?"

"Maybe. If I don't fall asleep first." He yawned again.

"And who will you pray for?"

After a pause the boy said, "Mum."

Mungo knew he should go away lest he disgrace himself utterly; but he could not. He did not believe in God but he still wanted to be included in his son's prayers.

"And Peggy, you'll not leave her out?"

"Oh, no."

Suddenly Mungo found himself panic-stricken. "And your brother," he shouted, "liar and scrounger that he is, you'll pray for him too?"

Billy began to sob. Dislike and defiance were in it, as well as fear.

"And for an old cat with a stink off him you'll pray?"

Then he recovered himself. "I'm sorry, son. I shouldn't have shouted at you. You're not to blame. Pray for whoever you like, leave out whoever you like."

In the hall, groaning, he stumbled over some marbles on the floor. He could imagine Bess yelling if she had stepped on them, "Is somebody trying to make a ballet dancer out of me?" Suddenly, in his imagination too, in his clutch almost, was the small bag in which he had kept his own marbles forty years ago. His aunt Kirstie had made it for him out of pink and white striped flannel, with a drawstring of tape.

60

Often, when unhappy, he had peeped in at his treasures, marbles or 'bools' of purple, green, and blue painted clay, glassies with swirls of mingled colours, indestructibles of glittering steel, and pale blood-alleys with their thin red veins. Yet why should these be associated in his imagination with Bess? They had all gone years before he had met her. By everything he had ever loved was he bound to her.

Leaving it all behind, his soul would be naked when he went to Myra. He was far from sure she would receive it as tenderly as it would need.

Wearily he went into the dark sitting-room and looked down into the street. Snow was still falling and beginning to lie. The multitude of flakes, swirling out of the blackness of the sky into the lamplight, reminded him of his fellow creatures, as numerous and evanescent. Some were dying, like old Hannah Gallie. Some were being born, some conceived. Some, like the Frasers upstairs, were making contented love. Some were playing whist, some whispering in public libraries. When they reached the ground the flakes became one with the others already fallen. Death, he thought, must be like that vast silent union.

The hope of Bess's being really ill flared up in his mind, and at the same instant the sky, and the snow-flakes in it, were for a few moments fierily red. It was only the glare from the blast furnaces at the steelworks but for its duration he pretended it was a sign. The men at work there, cloth-capped and tough-handed, would be talking about football, drink, wages, horses, and women. To see them as agents of God deserved the jocular blasphemy seldom out of their mouths. And yet as he kept staring at the sky and into his mind, both now dark again, he did see them or rather wanted to see them as such agents. Even the foulmouthed, the lecherous, and the cruel were given parts to play. No one was exempt, no one could claim conscientious objection. So he too was included.

Trying hard to be sincere and humble, he considered what his own part might be. It could be that he was to put his children to the test. Andrew had grown selfish, deceitful, and mercenary; Billy, child though he was, showed signs of guile and callousness; and Peggy's refusal to judge did not spring from love but from a disciplined neutrality. If he remained with them as their mother's degraded husband the relationship between him and them, and between themselves too, would go on deteriorating until in the end, not so far off either, there would be left as little true respect and faith as there was in most families after childhood. But if he fled with Myra, away from all this pretension and sour custom, they would be shocked into seeing not only him differently, but themselves and their mother. That hardening of vision which soon or late blinded most would have been prevented or at any rate delayed in them. They might suffer but it would redeem them.

There would be lesser repercussions. Colleagues at work, especially those collectors who came under his jurisdiction and who distrusted him as the official paid to harry them, would suddenly, as they gazed up at the cold dark sky or down at the dirty slush, start wondering. For the rest of their lives they would have learned that no man was completely knowable and therefore completely consumable, to be thrown away after use like a paper hankie; most importantly, each of them would have learned it about himself. Of course he did not expect them all to desert their wives and run off with well-to-do women to Spain. There were other ways of demonstrating that every man, however lowly in the world's hierarchies, was his own master, capable of surprising his Creator Himself.

Yes, much depended on him. If he shrank back now, no one would be saved; all, including Bess herself, would sink deeper into the morass.

62

8

EVEN IF HE had been there merely to retrieve her hat, knocked off several times getting her into the taxi and keeping her upright in it, Mr. Peffermill would have felt exploited; but in addition he had to bear the brunt of her stupefying weight, for Yuill the taxi-man, hearse-driver by trade, adept at humphing coffins, proved craftily useless at lifting and pushing a fat woman unboxed. Had Florence not been there Mr. Peffermill would have touched his hat, murmured a word or two of sympathy and advice, and then have made off with goloshed caution through the snow; but she was there, his betrothed more or less, looking to him for chivalry, and even brute strength. He had therefore to risk rupture, thrusting and heaving like a navvy. Nor was he recompensed when in the taxi Florence kissed him. There was as much passion in it as in a wren's flying on and off a twig. To make it ridiculous as well as inadequate there was monstrous Bess, supposed to be groaning and gasping her last, looking up from her spasms to stammer some insult about lovebirds. To punish her he meant, when helping her out of the taxi, to squeeze her behind painfully; but on the contrary she it was, by an accident worse than malice, who caught him with her elbow such a crack on the nose that, behind his squee-gee'd spectacles, his eyes flowed with tears. Inwardly he cursed her for a lump of creash and shit; outwardly, though, he accepted her slobbered apology with such gentlemanliness that Florence was pleased. Even Yuill, beer-sodden scullion of corpses, was impressed.

"I'll hurry on up," said Florence, "and get Niven to come

and help. Since it was him that got her into this state it's up to him to bear the burden of it."

"Do that, my dear," panted Mr. Peffermill. "He's a big fellow physically, more able to cope."

"Just you watch. Every time he touches her he grues. Just you watch."

She ran through the close and up the stairs.

"God, Bess," grunted Yuill, for the sixth time at least. "You're fairly having us on this night." He had her propped against the wall, Mr. Peffermill having stepped back for a breather.

"I don't know who's having who on, Bob," she muttered. "But I've got a pain here I can't stand much longer."

"Never underrate the human frame," counselled Mr. Peffermill. "It has remarkable powers of endurance."

"That's a comfort to know," said Yuill, sarcastic red-nosed dolt.

"I never could stand pain," whispered Bess. "As a wee lassie I had to be dragged to the dentist. You'll hae to drag me to the grave, Bob."

"By the time they come my way, Bess, they're willing enough. But you're miles off that yet. Though there's a damn draught blowing through here that's got double pneumonia in it."

"Whit's keeping Mungo?" she sobbed.

"He'll hae fallen asleep by the fire, wise man."

She tried to smile. "Wi' a book on his knee."

St. Augustine's Confessions, no doubt, thought Mr. Peffermill, with a sneer. Then he drew back, to watch closely as big Niven, in slippers and darned cardigan, hurried down the stairs, followed by Florence.

He went straight to his wife as if to rebuke or even strike her. When he spoke his tone was harsh; yet it could have been husbandly enough, for solicitude and love were not always mild-mouthed.

64

"What's this? What's this about?"

"Help me, Mungo," she whimpered.

It was pitiable, so fat a nymph appealing so meekly; and of course big Niven, true spouse of such a nymph, ought to have responded with some fond gibberish, and then have wracked his very testicles lugging her upstairs into the bed where she had so often borne his galloping weight. But to Mr. Peffermill's dumbfoundment the insurance inspector, supposed student of St. Augustine, said or rather snarled: "That's what I can't do. It's too late for that."

There was a pause.

"Well," muttered Yuill, "after more than a hundred funerals I thought nothing folk could say or do would ever surprise me. But I admit I'm surprised now."

Mr. Peffermill had to concur, with a titter.

"I'm not," said Florence.

Bess paid none of them any heed. She was trying to giggle, like a girl of eighteen. "You're playing me at my ain game, Mungo. I deserve it; ony time but this."

"Whatever this game is," said Yuill, "I'd like to suggest you get on wi' it in the warmth of your hoose. This draught would freeze the lugs off a brass monkey."

"Balls," whispered Mr. Peffermill, his own somehow tingling.

Niven's eyes looked mad. He banged his fist against the stone wall of the close.

"There's something I've got to say, before witnesses. I'm leaving you, Bess. Aye, for another woman. You've brought it on yourself."

There was another pause.

"Now that I've been a witness," muttered Yuill, "though to what Christ kens, I think I'll make myself scarce."

"What's the hurry?" cried Florence. "They're shut, long ago. Pay him, Ben."

c

Furious at her generosity with his money, Mr. Peffermill replied, with all the human feeling he could simulate: "Of course, my dear. How much?"

"Fifteen bob," said Yuill.

It was exorbitant, but Mr. Peffermill was in no position to argue. In any case by pleasing Florence now he might be buying himself a wealth of pleasure later.

Paid, Yuill made to leave. He ignored Niven, as one does a human mess that has no right to be public. "Cheer up, Bess," he said. "It'll turn oot to be nothing serious." He hurried away.

Mr. Peffermill noticed that Bess so far had not taken her husband's announcement seriously. She seemed to be in a daze of pain and reached out, smiling, for Niven; who kept back.

"There's worse than drink," said Florence, referring to Yuill. "There's murder."

There was indeed; and there was also death through pneumonia.

"I suggest," said Mr. Peffermill, "that whatever marital crisis our friends are involved in, the first thing is to get Bess, and ourselves, out of this freezing draught."

To be fair to Niven, after bashing her on the head with that cudgel of a threat, he now did more than his share in hoisting her up the stairs and into the house. She tried feebly to turn his holding of her into embraces, but he wouldn't have it.

Just inside the door she collapsed and lay sprawled on hands and knees, as helpless as a sow in labour. Her hat had come off again. As a matter of fact Mr. Peffermill had it in his hand.

A small boy in blue pyjamas appeared sleepily in the hall. As soon as Bess caught sight of him she began to wail: "Oh Christ, my weans, my poor weans."

Mr. Peffermill sought Niven's eyes; they were madder than ever. A mild man himself really by disposition, though implacable on principle, Mr. Peffermill was impressed. Niven had meant what he had said down in the close.

Florence bent over her friend. "Listen, Bess, what you need now is self-respect, especially in front of this poor wean."

Mr. Peffermill murmured: "Whatever's behind the scenes I suggest that Bess be put to bed and a doctor sent for. In the meantime I shall keep this boy company."

Lifting Bess into this high box bed might reveal what he had no right or wish to see. Female nakedness was only tolerable if it was beautiful; which, alas, was seldom. At home he had a pack of cards with on their backs coloured pictures of nude young women. In almost every case their breasts were so oversized as to be grotesque. He regretted it nightly.

"Well, boy," he said, when they were alone in the hall, "is there a warmer spot in the house?"

"I think the gas-fire's on in the sitting-room."

"Let's go there then."

The first thing Mr. Peffermill saw was not the gas-fire but a letter partly written on the table.

"Sit on the chair, boy, beside the fire. You're chittering."

He himself stood by the table, reading the letter.

"Is my mother sick?" asked the boy.

"She has a pain."

"Is it very bad?"

"Look for the silver lining, lad. Your mother's a big strong woman, isn't she? She's always joking, isn't she? She eats well. She's as heavy as a horse."

"But she fell and couldn't get up."

"She tripped; over that strip of wood that's there to keep out draughts. I'm sure you've tripped over it yourself."

"Sometimes."

"Well then, just think how much heavier your mother's legs are." So much so indeed they had brought her to that stumble called separation or divorce. But who, in St. Augustine's name, was this other woman for whom Niven was about to forsake the loyalties of twenty-five years? "With her I can be faithful to what is best in me. To stay here and go on being degraded would be cowardly."

"I wish Peggy was here."

Mr. Peffermill had forgotten the boy, fruit of that toppling marriage.

"Is she your sister?"

"Yes."

Mr. Peffermill too had a sister. He had not seen her for over fifteen years and did not pine. When he had been this boy's age he had been close enough to her. 'We twa hae paiddled in the burn.' Forty years of human existence could separate further than death itself.

Voices were heard out in the hall. The outside door opened and shut again. Someone had gone out. Then Florence came into the sitting-room. If ever a woman needed the mollifying of a fond cock it was she.

To the boy she spoke as sternly as if he was to blame. Thus were children made scapegoats. And why not, considering they were the products of what so often was the most deeply disappointing experience of their begetters?

"I think you should get back to bed," she said.

"Mrs. McTaggart," asked the child, "will Mum be all right?"

"We hope so, Billy. Your father's gone to phone for the doctor."

"The Frasers have got a phone."

The name seemed familiar to Mr. Peffermill. Was it not a Nan Fraser Niven was said to be having an affair with? Curious to use your fancy-woman's phone to bring a doctor to your wife.

"What's the matter with her?" asked the boy.

68

"If we knew that would we need a doctor?"

The boy looked as if the illogicality of that answer had struck him too. Surely the point of fetching a doctor was not just to find out what was wrong, but to have it cured?

"If you're going to be fit for school tomorrow you'd better get some sleep."

Again the child was not convinced. If his mother was seriously ill school tomorrow was unimportant. In him the masculine mind was at work. Women were incapable of appreciating tragedy: they were too concerned with continuity.

The boy slunk out.

At once Mr. Peffermill made for his betrothed and drew her close to him. She submitted, as usual not out of passion roused but out of policy formulated. Having agreed to marry him she would permit contact. He tested to find out how much and of what kind. His hand, pressed against her buttock, was allowed to remain, though the buttock itself shivered. His mouth on hers was given ten seconds' hospitality. But when his loins began thrusting, decorously enough, she objected. He was not too much annoyed or disappointed; after all testing was not performing.

"He's serious," she said, in joy. "He means it."

Mr. Peffermill considered that joy. Somehow he could not approve of it. "About leaving her?"

"Aye. It would be the best thing that could happen to her, poor soul."

"She doesn't seem to think so."

"She's always been blind to his selfishness and cruelty. But we saw it tonight down in the close, didn't we?"

"I doubt if she did."

"Even that sot Yuill was shocked. Well, she can't say I didn't warn her. He was at it again helping her into bed. If he'd taken an axe he couldn't have struck her crueller blows."

Mr. Peffermill could not help smiling. It was amusing enough just to picture Niven heaving her up first on to the chair by the side of the bed and then more or less rolling her into position. To imagine him in addition, as he panted and pushed, telling her he was leaving her for another woman was as droll a thing as had happened in that or any other living-room.

But he had to be loyal to his sex. "I hesitate to say this, Florence, knowing how attached to her you are. But the oaf may think he has a case, you know. Look at that letter."

Clinically he watched her as she read it.

She chewed her lips; murder was in her heart.

"I'm not surprised," she said when she dropped it on to the floor.

Mr. Peffermill picked it up and unobtrusively slipped it into his pocket. It would go into the drawer at home under his shirts, beside the playing cards.

"I've warned her," said Florence, "dozens of times. He's the biggest fraud in Glasgow, I've told her. He's deceiving you all the time. He hasn't a scrap of affection for you or the children. He's all for himself. She would never listen to me. Latterly she got quite angry and told me to be quiet. Now she knows who was right. God knows how many fancy women he's had all these years. No wonder he never had any money to give to her."

"But why run away with this particular fancy woman?"

"Because she'll have money, that's why."

Mr. Peffermill could not quite believe this. He also did not want to believe it. To escape with a wealthy woman was a stroke of luck Niven just did not deserve.

"Nonsense, my dear. No need to be cynical. Granted the affair's sordid, but what he says here could be true, you know. This woman may well bring out whatever good's in him."

"Are you excusing him, Ben Peffermill?"

"Not I, Florence. I am the lion that keeps its mate till death."

Then they heard Bess calling in desperation: "Mungo, Mungo, where are you? Please, Mungo, please, for God's sake."

"I'd rather see her stretched out dead," said Florence bitterly, "than listen to her plead with him. I'd better go to her."

"And am I just to sit here all alone? Shall I content myself with a book?"

"You'll find plenty. He's forever picking them up off barrows in the street. I doubt if he's ever read one in a hundred."

Though interested in the array of cheap-looking soiled volumes that Niven had had the ambition if not the capacity to read, and interested too to find out if *The Confessions of St. Augustine* was among them, Mr. Peffermill was at that moment still more interested in what Florence had to say to Bess. Therefore he went tiptoeing up to the living-room door. A floorboard creaked loudly, but if he had blown a trumpet the two women would not have heeded.

With a frankness that impressed but chilled him Florence was telling the sick woman some home truths indeed. Her voice had gone strangely deep, with that purely female resentment that even poor Chrissie's shrunken cords had been able to achieve now and then. "Aye, Bess, he's lain beside you in that very bed and schemed to desert you. He would never have had the courage to do it while you were fit and well and able for him; but the very moment he sees you stricken he kicks you in the face and in the place where your pain is. He should be libbed."

Bess wept, but in her tears there was no refreshment for the eavesdropper behind the door. For, suddenly as a light going out, interest died in Mr. Peffermill.

This had been happening more and more frequently in recent months. In the midst of some situation where others suffered and he merely watched he might have been expected to be the last to lose interest, especially as he was such an alert and subtle spectator. But no, still with the knife and fork in his hands, as it were, and the plate half full, appetite abruptly went. Apprehensive about seeking reasons, he had ventured so far as to fancy it might be in some necromantic way Chrissie punishing him from the grave. So often had he pretended to listen sympathetically to her thin incessant havers, but really with his mind feasting on more substantial matters. In the end she had realised she might as well be talking to, as she rather curiously put it, a stone statue of Christ. True to her nature she had at the time appeared to bear him no ill-will, but was she not now, in the grave, like one of Dracula's vampire daughters, sucking the marrow out of his mind? The thought was fantastic, but were not certain statues of Christ reputed to ooze blood?

He left, without letting Florence know. Going down the stairs he met Niven coming up, with unmelted snow on his moustache and madness still in his eyes. Curiosity ought to have been as busy as a ferret in a rabbit warren, but Mr. Peffermill could not be bothered even to inquire if the doctor was coming.

Niven, on the contrary, was desperate to speak. "As one of my witnesses, Mr. Peffermill," he said, "you are owed an explanation."

"Excuse me, Mr. Niven, I take care that no man ever owes me anything, not even explanations."

At the mouth of the close he paused for a few seconds looking out at the snow, and remembering a story he had read about a trapper with a broken leg, who, shut in by blizzards, had day by day starved to death, after trying to find nourishment in animal skins and wood.

9

OFTEN ENOUGH DURING the war Mungo had felt fiercely and exaltedly contemptuous of his enemies and of those on his own side hampered by scruples. Afterwards, almost ashamed of the wary respect shown him by men who had seen him fight so ruthlessly, he had justified himself by the simple but incontrovertible argument that in war if one's cause was just and necessary then one's enemies had either to be forced to submit or killed without mercy.

Now for the first time in peace that ferocity of principle was impelling him. Yuill's stupid disgust, Peffermill's smirking disapproval, Flo McTaggart's hatred, and poor Billy's terror were all admirable on Bess's behalf, but so had the courage and patriotism of the Germans he had helped to slaughter been admirable on their country's behalf. Striding from one corpse in field-grey uniform to another, he had been able to tell them all, the grey-haired and the still unshaved, that their burst bellies and blown off heads had been necessary for the freedom of mankind. And today no-one, not even the fathers and mothers, or widows and children, of those butchered Germans dared to say he had not been right. Well, tonight, in this house where his own children had been conceived and born, he was having to be savage and remorseless again, in defence of another kind of freedom more important even than the other, only this time the enemies he had to overcome, at whatever cost, were his children and their mother.

When he had rushed down into the close to find Bess held up against the wall by Yuill as if she was being raped, he had

had a rifle in his hands again and had not hesitated to fire it. From that moment Bess was as good as dead for him. It was her corpse he had carried upstairs and lifted into bed.

The doctor, Yellowlees' assistant, was young and zealous, but puzzled both by the patient's symptoms and by her husband's peculiar fervour. Mungo noticed him discreetly sniffing, as if he suspected drink. Fiddling with his stethoscope, he suggested it would be safer to have her removed to hospital.

"That's for you to say," said Mungo.

Bess by this time was quiet with exhaustion, amazement, and despair.

Over at the fireplace the doctor whispered, "I ought to warn you, Mr. Niven, this looks as if it could be pretty serious."

For answer Mungo took the silver eagle down from the mantelpiece. "Do you see this?"

The doctor was glad of the momentary diversion. "German?"

"Aye. Do you know how I got it?"

"Trophy of war, I suppose?"

"Call it that. It's nothing great, is it? I doubt if it's worth more than ten pounds. But do you know what it represented, and still does?"

The doctor was now uneasy. "German rapacity, I suppose."

"No. Not to me. German timidity and humbleness."

"You don't say?"

"Yes, I do say. I took it, by force, from a house where two German women, one old enough to be my mother, sat smiling and tried to convince us it was a terrible mistake, all this killing and raping and torturing, that the Germans were really at heart timid and humble people."

"I see." Though comparatively inexperienced, the doctor

was not unaccustomed to eloquence on the part of patients' spouses or friends. Mostly, though, it was of the one kind, thankfulness at death averted or pain relieved. Grief, he had found, was inclined to be tongue-tied. This was certainly the first time he had encountered, at the bedside of a seriously ill woman, political passion, out-of-date at that, on the part of her husband. It could be of course the way anxiety affected the man.

"I'll telephone right away, Mr. Niven. The ambulance should be here inside half an hour."

Mungo saw him to the door, and so was there to see Peggy come trudging up the stairs.

She was soaked and downcast. "Was that Dr. Yellowlees' assistant?"

"It was."

"What was he doing here? Is Billy sick?"

"Not Billy."

"Mum?"

"Yes."

He noticed her freeze. Even the fit of coughing that had started stopped at once. Her eyes were closed. She shivered. On her thin face was not only anxiety for her mother but also a curious acceptance that frightened him.

"It must be serious to need a doctor at this time of night."

"He's young, Peggy, but—yes, he thinks it might be serious."

"Is it this pain Mum's been complaining about?"

"It seems so. She never complained to me."

"No."

He gripped her arm. "Peggy, before you go in to see your mother there's something I've got to tell you."

"Whatever it is it can't be more important than Mum's illness."

But she waited.

75

"You must have noticed that for some time I've not been happy here. I'm not going to blame anybody. We're all victims of our own natures. Probably I'm as much to blame myself as anybody."

"I think I should go and see Mum."

"I've decided to leave her, Peggy. For all our sakes, hers as well. You may condemn me now. Later, when you're older, when you've had more experience, you'll understand. You have imagination."

"Let me go, please."

"You're soaked. You'd better take this coat off first."

She shook her head.

"Peggy, for God's sake, try to be fair to me. Nobody else in this house will. You've seen and heard what I've had to put up with. You've watched all my ambitions mocked."

Again she shook her head, meaning he did not know what. He had to let her go. Still wearing her soaked coat, she went into the living-room.

He hesitated and then followed her.

Flo McTaggart was standing by the fire warming her hands.

In bed Bess seemed unconscious. Her face was pale and flabby with suffering.

"How is she, Mrs. McTaggart?" whispered Peggy.

Flo shrugged her shoulders. "How is any woman that's been murdered?"

Peggy glanced at her father.

"Aye, Peggy, murdered," repeated Flo. "Words can kill."

Peggy went over to the bed. "Hello, Mum," she said. "This is Peggy? What's happened? How are you feeling?"

Her mother opened her eyes. "You speak to him, Peggy," she whispered. "He'll listen to you. He's always been a bit afraid of you. You've been too cool, you see."

"Cool?" The girl smiled.

"But no cheek, mind, no impudence. He's your faither and always will be. Tell him I admit I've been at fault. I've joked when I should hae shown respect. But it was always oot o' affection. I thought he knew that. Tell him that, Peggy."

"I don't think there's any need to tell him, Mum. He knows."

"See, that's what I meant by saying you've always been too cool. I want you to tell him. None of you is to take sides against him. Flo's bitter. She always has been. But none of you has ony right to be bitter. He's always been a good faither to you."

"Tell her, Peggy," said Flo, "she shouldn't be talking. The doctor said she'll need every ounce of her strength."

"Where is he?" whispered Bess. "Flo said he'd gone for the doctor."

"He's here, Mum. The doctor's been and gone."

"Has he? I never noticed. Peggy, would you and Flo mind going oot for a minute or twa? I would like to talk to your faither alone."

"All right, Mum." Peggy turned away from the bed.

"I understand," snapped Flo, and marched out.

"I have nothing to say to her, Peggy. I warn you I have nothing to say."

Peggy went out too.

"Mungo," called Bess weakly. "Are you there?"

"I'm here."

"Come over where I can see you. That's no' asking too much, is it?"

It almost was. But to refuse would be to start retreating. So he stepped boldly forward to the bed he had shared with her for years. He remembered where and when she had bought the curtains that draped it; he could have described the shopkeeper and given his name. But this was the kind of knowledge that could betray him, and his mind was full of it.

77

Standing over her, he remembered visiting her in the Maternity Hospital soon after Billy was born. The woman in the next bed, sitting up talking to her husband, had leaned over too far and revealed her naked buttocks. Never had a revelation been less lust-provoking. Tenderness towards all women had flowed from his love for his wife, and for their new-born son.

And she was gazing at him with the same love as she had done then, only this time the jocularity in it was replaced by humility.

"Tell me you were joking, Mungo," she whispered. "It's just not in your nature to be happy wi' anither woman, in anither place. This is your hame, Mungo. We are your family."

Like the Lord he hardened his heart.

"I ken I've never been the kind of wife you needed. I've tried, but no' very hard. It would hae been useless. I'm juist the kind of woman I am. But I did think, maist o' the time, that if we werenae perfect for each ither, at least we'd proved in twenty-five years that we'd do."

"The doctor said you weren't to talk."

"You were joking about this ither woman?"

How easy to have lied and said yes, he had been joking. In half an hour she would be in hospital, where the lie might give her a day or two's comfort. But he felt he must tell the truth.

"I was not joking."

"Aye, you were, Mungo."

"Think what you like."

"What's she like then?"

"I'm not going to talk about it."

"But what about oor weans, Mungo?"

"They're not weans any longer."

"They still need looking after. What's going to happen to

78

them, you away and me in hospital? What's going to happen to oor family?"

"They'll be all right."

"Who's going to do it? My family can hardly afford to look after themselves. And we are a' the family you've ever had."

"I'm aware of my obligations."

"But how could you manage it oot of your wages, Mungo? It was always a tight enough squeeze as it was. Not that I ever grumbled. Did I ever grumble, Mungo?"

She had, often enough, in her so-called humorous way. But he preferred to say nothing: it was the only dignified thing to do.

"But I wasn't only thinking aboot money, Mungo. There's Andrew. Who's going to stop him making a mess of his life by marrying that papish McKenzie girl?"

"He's old enough to look after himself."

"But he's so easily led, Mungo. Those McKenzies will capture him, you'll see."

"It could be the girl loves him, and would make him a good wife."

"Never." She began to weep. "I'd raither see him deid first. But what effect is it going to hae on him, seeing you leave me like this? You were always preaching at him aboot right and wrang."

"And got laughed at."

"But, Mungo, you were like a wean wanting toys its parents couldn't afford."

He could not help saying bitterly, "You're condemning yourself out of your own mouth."

"If I've ever stood in your way, Mungo, it was frae fondness. Remember that first day, on the St. Columba, sailing to Rothesay? I said to Flo, 'That's the man I'm going to marry.' Mind how I bumped into you, by accident I made oot."

He remembered it too well. But that tall dark-haired finely-shaped laughing girl was dead and buried long ago, just as the St. Columba with its famous black and red funnels was broken up. All the same, that first meeting among the seagulls opposite Toward Lighthouse had been happier with more exciting promise than his first meeting with Myra at the symphony concert in St. Andrew's Hall. He couldn't tell what music had been played that evening, nor what Myra had been wearing, though it was only a few months ago. But on the steamer the band of two fiddles and a concertina had been playing a medley of Scots airs, among them his Auntie Kirstie's favourite, 'The Rowan Tree,' and the big vivacious red-cheeked girl had been wearing a red and white dress.

"You always were the first with me, Mungo. You always will be, wherever you are, whatever you're doing. To come hame at night and find you waiting, wi' the kettle on for tea, that was the height of happiness."

It was unbearable. She was his enemy who had degraded him; yes, but she had loved him, and perhaps still did. Could love, other than self-love, ever be degrading? Had he blamed her for a degradation that had been inevitable?

When he went away from the bed he felt he needed someone to consult, someone whose judgment he could trust. But as always there was no one, not even Peggy; and in any case he could hear her in Billy's room, comforting her brother. It was hardly likely that her comforting would include an extenuation of their father's cruelty towards their mother. For of course cruelty it was.

"But sometimes," he muttered, as he stood in the hall, "it's necessary to be cruel."

A world that accepted the necessity of war and its evils must agree with him. So must Flo McTaggart who wanted criminals flogged. So must Bess who would never consent to Andrew's marrying the Catholic girl. But Peggy might not.

He had never known her to do a cruel thing, or countenance cruelty in others. Trembling, he found himself praying she could not change, that her resolution would be strengthened rather than weakened by his example.

For his part, like Columbus he had made his decision and must sail on.

10

FOUR DAYS LATER, on Sunday, Peggy was combing
Billy's hair, getting him ready to go and visit their mother in
hospital. Spikes at the back of his head could not be subdued;
nor could an awkwardness in his mind.

"Mum could get it to stay down," he said dourly.

"Yes." Staring at his sullen face in the mirror Peggy
scarcely recognised her carefree young brother of less than a
week ago. Up to now he had kept his opinions and emotions
to himself, about their mother's illness and their father's
desertion; or almost so, for this insistence that his mother
could do everything for him better than anyone else was an
indication of his desperate need of her. She could boil eggs
exactly as he liked them, and fix his tie as it ought to be, as
well as brush his hair properly.

Suddenly he said, with a viciousness that appalled her,
"When they catch him will they put him in jail?"

She could just shake her head.

"Well, they should."

She did not know whether she had a right to rebuke him.
Few would ever blame him if for the rest of his life he despised
his father. One person would, though, the most important
person in the world: their mother.

"Don't talk like that, Billy. Mum wouldn't like it."

"Auntie Beat says he should be put in a cage in the street
so that people could throw stones and rotten eggs at him."

Aunt Beatrice was their mother's sister, fat, kind-hearted
enough, but with a ghetto mind.

"She had no right to say such a thing to you."

"Is Mum going to die?"

"No, of course not."

"Everybody says so. Andrew, Aunt Beat, Uncle Will, and Uncle Dave."

Uncle Will and Uncle Dave were their mother's brothers. Their father's lack of relations had been very noticeable these past few days.

"I'm sure they never said anything of the kind, Billy Niven."

"They all think it. I wish it was him that was going to die."

"Nobody's going to die. Except poor Mrs. Gallie; and she's very old."

"I never liked him."

"Mum would be angry if she heard you say that. And it's not true."

"It is true. He wouldn't let us get television."

"We couldn't afford it, Billy."

"That's stupid. Tom McDonald and James Dalglass have it, and they're poorer than us."

"Well, Dad wanted us all to read books. Besides, he bought you football boots."

"Because Mum made him."

They both knew the truth was their mother had protested against it as an extravagance they couldn't afford.

"He helped you with your homework."

"And I wished he wouldn't. Because he couldn't. He didn't know French or geometry. He left school at fourteen. All those books in the bookcase through in the sitting-room, he couldn't even read them and they're in English. He would take one, look at it, and then put it back. He'd do that with half a dozen. Then he'd sit down with one and try to read it, but after a wee while he'd drop it and read a newspaper instead. Mrs. McTaggart said he was a fraud. So he was."

Peggy was amazed and horrified. With what malevolent

closeness must this young brother of hers have watched their father. She could imagine her other brother saying to him: "Good for you, Billy. By Christ, he was a fraud. Remember all those times he would talk about raising the value of humanity. He was at it that very night. And all the time he was getting ready to rush off and leave us without a penny."

Andrew, with justice, she supposed, was particularly bitter about the financial position.

"You're greeting," said Billy, in accusation almost.

So she was, as she found when she put her hand to her cheeks.

"You said Mum wasn't going to die."

She shook her head and tried to smile.

"Then what are you greeting for?"

For so many things. For Billy himself turning corrupt before her eyes. For Robert Logan sleeping every night with big-breasted Maud. For Andrew given sanction to act as callously towards Ishbel McKenzie as suited him. For their mother drugged to escape pain and the terror of death. And above all for their father, amidst whose falseness and hypocrisy had been yearnings for something beyond the humdrum fish-and-chips, kettle-on-the-hob, football-coupon, telly-watching, whist-playing bookless existence so satisfactory to Aunt Beat and all the other typical ghetto-dwellers, including, it had to be said, their mother.

"It's time we left," she said. "We don't want to be late, do we?"

Outside in the street icy rain was falling. The gutters were still thick with slush. On the way to the bus-stop they met Mr. and Mrs. Fraser, walking arm-in-arm under the one umbrella. Peggy wanted to hurry past, but Mrs. Fraser stopped them. Despite her soft smiling face and the perfumed glove that touched Billy so pityingly on the cheek, she did not seem sincerely concerned about her neighbour dying in

84

hospital. She and her husband seemed more interested in their other neighbour who, by his terrible act of treachery and hate, had made their own loving and trust in each other as valuable as money in the bank.

Mrs. Fraser whispered in Peggy's ear. "And has there been no news from your father? Mr. Fraser and I thought that since your mother's so ill he would have changed his mind. No? Tut, tut, how awful." But she could not help smiling.

Mr. Fraser had been having a few brave words with Billy about football, and his last gesture, when they parted, was to thrust up his thumb.

Billy, Peggy saw, was pleased with them. They, and Aunt Beat, and Uncle Will, were the kind of people he would want to be like. Again she felt a pang of guilty sympathy for her father. To escape from the darkness of the ghetto-mind, especially if you had been imprisoned in it for over forty years, you had to be ruthless as well as reckless. Whether you were to be condemned or congratulated would depend on what use you made of your freedom.

When Billy took her hand at the bus-stop she knew that she too was a traitor, ready to escape when the chance came.

This feeling of imminent treachery was strengthened when they went into the hospital waiting-room and found their uncles and aunts already there, wrapped up in raincoats and, still more impenetrably, in grim respectability and crass prejudice.

Aunt Beatrice, big and stout like their mother, gave Billy a tearful hug. She was always ready to weep and seemed to enjoy it. Her sister Bess often teased her. "Remember how you wept because there wasn't enough steak pie to go round at oor mither's funeral? You swore Shaw the butcher had cheated us." Aunt Beatrice was always thinking someone had cheated her.

Uncle Dave was the one Peggy liked best. Tall and bald,

85

he needed spectacles but his small tight-mouthed wife Sadie would not allow him to wear them outside. "You might not mind looking like a fool, Dave Aitchison, as well as talking like one, but I do." So he stumbled over gutters and into lamp-posts. Nevertheless he remained so amiable that Mrs. McTaggart dismissed him as half-witted. He sought always to find good in people, not because he was a Christian for he never went to church, but because it was simply a seeking he had been born with.

"I'm still trying to understand it, Peggy," he whispered to her. "I always thought your faither was a superior sort of man."

Aunt Sadie, suspicious as ever, thrust her sharp ears forward. "Superior at cruelty, you mean?" she snapped.

She always reminded Peggy of Mrs. McTaggart and Ishbel McKenzie's mother: small, neat, tight-mouthed, wary-eyed, purse-clutching women who, after long years of resistance to the degradations of ghetto poverty, could not relax now though they were not so hard-pressed as before. For people like Maggie Ralston and Robert Logan's family, still under harsh siege, they had no pity; these, they said, had always been too ready to give in.

Uncle Will was small, fidgety, and slightly deaf. He had a habit of always agreeing with himself, because, so his sister Bess said, nobody else could be bothered agreeing with him. Certainly he took care never to say anything that wasn't utterly obvious.

"If Niven had taken a dagger and stabbed poor Bess in the back," he now said, in his querulous squeaky voice, "he couldn't be mair responsible for her daith. Aye."

"But Mum's not dead," said Billy.

They were instantly sad for the boy's sake. Uncle Will slipped half a crown into his pocket, Aunt Sadie straightened his tie, and Aunt Beatrice stroked his wet hair.

86

"Medical science performs miracles these days," said Uncle Dave. "And Bess has been strong all her life."

Uncle Peter, Aunt Beatrice's husband, was a stout, reddish, freckled man with eager stupid eyes. Catching sight of him from the window, his sister-in-law more than once had cried: "Oh, my God, under the bed everybody. Here comes Peter. Whit's it going to be this time? Last time it was slot machines in gents' toilets that don't work."

This morning it was the theory that Mungo Niven must have taken a mad turn.

"Otherwise," he said, "how are you going to explain it? To leave hoose, weans, wife, and work withoot a word o' explanation to onybody. I would not be surprised if in a day or twa they dragged him oot o' the Clyde. Something that happened in the war could hae caused it. He was in the thick of the fighting, you ken. Delayed shock, or something."

"Ken this?" said Aunt Sadie. "If he turned up this minute, bold as brass, wi' that moustache o' his scented, they'd let him in to see poor Bess."

Uncle Will's wife, Aunt Nellie, seldom spoke, and always kept nodding to what everybody else said even if they were contradicting one another.

"He's her man," she observed. "In the eyes of the law he's still her closest kin."

"And in the eyes of God, you might say," said Uncle Dave.

His wife wished to rebuke him for this typical imbecility, but she could not quite find the words. "If that is so," she said instead, "then God will ken how to deal with him."

"Where's Andrew?" sobbed Aunt Beatrice.

"He's coming," said Peggy.

"Oh, you don't have to tell me that. I ken Andrew will come to see his poor mither. He's always been very fond of her. Even as a wean, Peggy, he was always that bit softer-hearted than you."

87

"Bess always enjoyed her food," remarked Uncle Will. "Aye. And damn the consequences. Aye."

Then a Sister arrived and roused indignation by announcing that since Mrs. Niven was very ill and under sedation the doctor had decided that only her very closest kin should be allowed in to see her that morning.

"I'm her sister," said Aunt Beatrice. "Is that no' close enough?"

"Not quite, I'm afraid. The doctor said her husband and her children."

"She must be gey bad. Aye," said Uncle Will.

"Have we been sitting here for nothing then?" snapped Aunt Sadie.

"I kent Niven would be let in," observed Aunt Nellie, nodding.

"Is Mr. Niven here?" asked the Sister.

"No," snapped Aunt Sadie. "And no' likely to be either."

"I see. Are these her children?"

"Yes," said Peggy, quietly.

"Right. Please follow me then. As for you others, please realise it's for the patient's own good. We all want to give her every chance, don't we?"

"Not us all," retorted Aunt Beatrice, though she was sobbing. "There's one praying she'll dee."

The Sister raised her pencilled brows but said nothing. She patted Billy on the head and then went off. Peggy and Billy followed.

Going up the stairs Peggy whispered, "Maybe I should go in first."

"We'll go in together," he said, at his dourest.

They were led to one of the small private rooms for serious cases. Peggy noticed the surreptitious glances of sympathy cast at them by other patients and visitors. Outside the door was a table at which another Sister sat, as if on guard. She was young, pretty, and fair-haired. A few moments ago she had been laughing with a doctor. Now she switched on a business-like concern.

"I suppose these are Mrs. Niven's children, Sister?"

"Yes. Over to you then, Sister."

"Well," said the fair-haired one cheerfully, "your mother's expecting you. Isn't your father with you?"

"No. But my other brother will be here shortly." Peggy dropped her voice. "Is it all right for Billy to see her? Every time we've phoned we've been told she's very ill."

"So she is, I'm afraid. She's having a pretty serious operation tomorrow. At present she's under treatment and you may find her not too clear in her mind. As for your brother seeing her, yes, I think he should, for a minute or two anyway."

"I want to," said Billy.

"But don't have her talking too much. It's a pity your father hasn't managed to come. She seemed to be looking forward to his visit. Of course he hasn't been here before, has he?"

"We don't know," said Peggy. "Has he?"

"I'm afraid not. I believe he's telephoned, though. Is there trouble?"

Peggy nodded.

"That's a pity. Well, let's go in, shall we?" She opened the door. "Mrs. Niven, two young persons to see you."

Peggy heard Billy gasp. He had thought his mother was already dead. In the white nightgown, with her hands clasped above the sheet, her eyes shut, and her face sagging, she was not like their mother at all. Her hair looked as white as the pillow.

The Sister went out. Moments later Peggy heard her talking in an ordinary voice to a colleague.

Billy stared round the little room, as if hoping to see some

89

miraculous apparatus or medicine that would save his mother's life. There was nothing, except a wash-hand basin, a chair, and a locker with a glass of water on it.

They were not sure their mother knew they were there. Then she whispered, still with her eyes closed. "Has there been ony message?"

"No, Mum," said Peggy, "there hasn't."

With a great effort their mother opened her eyes and looked at Billy. She even tried to smile. "Who managed to put a shed like that in your hair?" she asked.

"Peggy," he said, as if angrily. "Peggy."

"What kind of comb did she use? It must have been a horse's."

"It was the big blue one."

That comb then represented their home. They had all used it.

"Is she looking after you all right?"

"She makes me go to school."

"I should say so. I'd be chasing you doon the stairs myself wi' a whip."

"But she didn't go herself on Wednesday or Thursday."

"Not frae choice, I'm sure. Poor Peggy. Are you getting the brunt o' all this?"

"No. You've got dozens of friends, Mum. People I don't know stop me in the street and ask after you and offer to help."

For a few moments their mother was silent.

"Is old Hannah gone yet?" she asked.

"No."

"You'll see, I'll be gone before her after all."

"You mustn't say that, Mum. Andrew will be here soon."

Their mother's voice became a whine. "Poor Andrew. How is he taking things, Peggy? He always was too sensitive for his own good."

That was a mother's judgment, thought Peggy. The truth

90

was Andrew was taking things in his usual way, blaming everybody but himself, and wanting to know what they were going to do for money.

"Like the rest of us, Mum, he's doing his best in the circumstances."

"So am I, Peggy. There's been a dozen experts and specialists poking at me inside and oot. They've made up their minds. I'm for the butcher tomorrow. I had to sign the paper myself."

"Will you be better after this operation?" demanded Billy.

"That's the idea onyway, son. Then I'll be back oot in no time, eating a' the crispest chips straight oot o' the pan."

He smiled. That was a humorous grumble of his.

"But why didn't Andrew come wi' you two?" she asked.

"He's with Ishbel McKenzie," said Billy, scowling at Peggy.

She had asked him not to mention Ishbel. But like his mother he did not approve of her, because she was a Catholic. He said Catholic children jeered and threw stones at him and his friends.

Their mother's fingers writhed on the sheet.

"He said he was going to bring her here to see you," added Billy.

"Here? He couldnae do that."

"Of course not," said Peggy. "You know how Billy gets things mixed up. But you haven't told us how you're feeling, Mum."

"You can see for yourself how I'm feeling."

"You're going to have dozens of visitors once you're able to see them."

"I don't want to see onybody. Not even Flo. She's too bitter. Are you sure there's been no message? He telephones every day." She began to weep.

"Aunt Beatrice and all the others are downstairs, Mum."

"Everybody will be there in the end but me."

"Don't talk like that, Mum. We need you. You've got to come home again."

"A few sticks of furniture and a blue comb don't make a home."

Peggy was silent. She was too accustomed to seeing her mother as a mother or as a wife, cooking meals and mending clothes. Even now it was difficult to see her as a woman deeply in love with a man.

"Is there anything you'd like us to bring you, Mum?"

"You ken what I'd like you to bring me."

"Tell us, Mum," said Billy eagerly, "and we'll bring it. Is it Lucozade? If it is we've brought a bottle. Look, it's in the bag. We didn't know if you'd get eating sweeties but we brought some chocolate caramels. We knew you liked them."

"So did he."

Billy at last understood. He scowled as if he thought he had been duped.

"Maybe I should cast him out of my mind, as Flo says. Maybe I should never forgive him. Maybe I should refuse to my dying day ever to see or hear of him again. I ken that what he's done to me is as cruel a thing as was ever done by one being to another; and I don't think I deserved it. But if it had been a hundred times mair cruel I would still want him back."

"You've not to get excited, Mum."

"Look for him, Peggy. Go to the police. They'll find him. He's still in Glesca. Tell him where I am."

"He knows where you are, Mum."

Her mother stared up at her for one terrible moment with what was undeniably dislike. "You always had a hard streak in you, Peggy. Some day you'll be fond of a man yourself. Then you'll understand."

"I think I understand now, Mum."

"No, you don't. Whatever happens, remember this; tell

them all this: I was prood to be his wife, right to the end."

Then she closed her eyes and tightened her lips.

"I think we should go now, Billy," said Peggy.

He nodded miserably. For him the visit would be continued in nightmares.

Peggy bent over their mother. "Mum, we're going now. We'll be back. Get well. Please get well."

The Sister opened the door and looked in.

Peggy nodded. "We're just going. Cheerio, Mum. We'll be back as soon as we can."

Billy was at the door when he turned, ran back to the bed, and kissed his mother. Like Peggy, she was surprised. Kissing was not common in their family. As they left, their mother was weeping.

Outside the Sister whispered to Peggy, "You know, Miss Niven, it would help a lot if your father could come."

"Yes."

"Is there any possibility?"

"I don't know."

"I see. Well, it's a great pity."

"Yes, it is. Come on, Billy. Thank you, Sister."

Going down the stairs Peggy stopped.

"I know what you're going to say," said Billy. "I've to tell them nothing."

She hadn't quite meant that. Or had she? "Well, it's really just our business, Billy."

"I like Aunt Beat," he said. "If she asks me I'll tell her."

"She'll ask you all right."

"Then I'll tell her."

They had been invited to Aunt Beatrice's for lunch. Billy was going, but Peggy had declined.

When she made to take his hand he would not let her. He and Andrew were Aitchisons, according to Aunt Beatrice; she, Peggy, was a Niven.

11

WORRIED THOUGH HE was about his mother, Andrew could not help grinning at the expected horror on the faces of his uncles and aunts when he came into the waiting-room with Ishbel.

Even Uncle Dave, so fair-minded he thought Celtic sometimes deserved to win, had confessed he was never happy in the presence of Catholics: they had a different sort of smell off them, hard to describe, but with candles in it somewhere. That they prayed for the dead did not offend him as it did Aunt Beatrice, but that they thought their prayers would do any good did, in some obscure way. So when he caught sight of Ishbel he smiled politely but his peering eyes were sad and puzzled.

The others' eyes were keen, angry, and knowing. They saw in Ishbel subtle sinister papish slyness, as his mother did. As a labourer's daughter and a grocer's assistant, it was bad enough of her to aspire to a University student who would soon be a teacher without her at the same time having her Catholic claws in his soul, ready to make it turn.

Aunt Sadie brought up the subject of his father. "As you can see, Andrew, he's no' here. I hope you realise just what it is he has done."

He nodded.

"You're the head of your family now, Andrew."

Another nod.

"We've been wondering whether this might mean you having to leave the University."

If he had to leave it would not break their hearts. They

thought he should never have gone there in the first place. None of their sons and daughters, his cousins, had advanced beyond the third form at school. He had his father to thank for his opportunity.

Then Peggy and Billy came in. At once Andrew hurried across to them, taking Ishbel with him.

"Hello, Peggy," he said. "You see, I've brought Ishbel."

She smiled at Ishbel in a friendly way but said, "You shouldn't have."

He sneered. "You smitten with prejudice too, Peg? I'd never have believed it."

"It's got nothing to do with prejudice. Mum mustn't be upset, that's all. She's very ill."

"I don't want to cause any trouble," murmured Ishbel.

"Then go away." It was Billy who said that, fists clenched. "Mum doesn't want to see you."

"Did she say that?" asked Andrew, grinning.

"Yes, she did."

"The Sister said Mum had to be kept as calm as possible," said Peggy. "She's to go through a serious operation tomorrow."

"I'm very sorry to hear that," whispered Ishbel.

Then Billy saw Aunt Beatrice waving to him. He went over to her.

It was Ishbel's chance. "You see, Peggy, Andrew and I will have to get married, so we thought we should come and get your mother's blessing."

Andrew winked.

"Are you pregnant?" asked Peggy.

"Quick on the uptake, our Peggy," said Andrew.

Though ashamed, Ishbel was proud too, and pleased.

"It's got nothing to do with me," said Peggy, "except that I don't want Mum hurt more than she is already. She's dangerously, ill you know."

"That's why I thought, why Andrew and me thought, we ought to tell her." Ishbel looked determined.

Andrew winked again, but Peggy, cool, shrewd, perceptive Peggy, understood no better than fat-witted Aunt Beat had.

"It's my business, Peg," he said. "As Aunt Sadie has just said I'm head of the family now. Trust me. I can handle this."

"I hope so." With a smile at Ishbel Peggy walked away.

Going up the stairs Ishbel was anxious to be sure she ought to see his mother.

"Leave it to me," he said. "I know what I'm doing."

She gave him a grateful, loving smile.

The fair-haired Sister at the table outside his mother's door stared hard at Ishbel.

He showed his visitor's card. "I'm Andrew Niven. I've come to see my mother."

"Yes, Mr. Niven. But who's the young lady? Only very close members of the family are being admitted. Doctor's orders, strictly enforced."

"We're going to get married," whispered Ishbel.

"I see. Well, I suppose you come into the category, don't you? But you mustn't stay long. No more than five minutes."

"Will it be all right if Ishbel stays out here until I prepare my mother?"

"If you wish." Sister indicated a chair for Ishbel to sit on. He noticed her noticing that Ishbel had no engagement ring.

He went in. His mother lay awake. From the way her hands were clasped on her breast and her legs straight out she seemed to be playing at being dead. He knew he was right when she turned and saw him. She was so desperately glad then to find herself still alive. Tears of relief and love tumbled down her cheeks. She held out a hand that inside a few days had shrunk to half its size. The veins in her wrist were as blue as forget-me-nots.

96

Taking her hand, he sat down beside her. "How are you, Mum?" he asked, hoarse because of the lump in his throat. "How's it going, then?"

She tried to smile. "Not too well, son. I hear auld Hannah's still cheating them."

"And you're going to cheat them too."

"God bless you, son. You're greeting like a wean. Peggy now, she finds it hard to greet. She always has done, even when she was a tot."

"Aye, always the wee stoic, our Peg."

She tightened her grip of his hand. "Andrew, I lie here dreading I'll never see you and Billy and Peggy again, and it crushes my he'rt."

"You'll be seeing the three of us around for the next forty years."

"I'd be over eighty then."

"And I'll be over sixty."

"You'd hae grandweans."

"Here, I'd have to get married first."

"Come closer, son. Make sure you marry one of your own kind. And to help you on in the world choose her frae among the clever lassies you ken at the University. This McKenzie girl, she's not for you. Billy was saying something daft aboot you bringing her here to see me."

"Now keep the heid, Mum, as we say in Glesca. She's outside."

"Wha?"

"Ishbel."

"In the street, you mean?"

"No. Outside this room. Now don't get excited. Just let me tell you why I've brought her. You'll think it's good news."

"I hope so, son."

"You see, Mum, it's like this. For weeks I've been trying to tell her it's no good her and me going on. You would never

D   97

approve, and I would never marry anybody against your will; just as she'd never marry anybody against her mother's will. But she just won't believe me. She thinks I'm at the kidding. So I thought if I brought her here you could tell her yourself. But please, Mum, do it as gently as you can. She's fond of me, you know."

"It's for your ain good, son."

"I know that."

"Lying here, Andrew, I've thought about it. And it wouldn't do. It never does. These Catholics want everything. If I was to be promised my life for it, Andrew, I juist couldnae gie you and her my blessing."

"Well, if that's how you feel here's your chance to tell her. You'll be doing me a good turn too. Will I bring her in?"

"Juist a minute, son. Andrew, I want you to find your faither and bring him back to me. I asked Peggy but she was neutral, she's always been neutral. I'm asking you, Andrew. Find him and explain."

He did not know what he was to explain. "I'll do my best, Mum. But I'd better bring Ishbel in before our time's up."

"Andrew, I'd raither you didn't. I don't want to speak to her."

"It'll take only a minute."

"You'll stay in here with us? You'll no' leave us alone?"

"I'll be here."

As he wriggled his hand out of hers and went to the door he thought there was one thing anyway he could say to his father if he ever met him again: Admire me, Dad. Praise me. Look how quickly I've learned to follow your example.

Ishbel jumped up when she saw him.

He shook his head. "I'm not sure. She's confused, you see. I think she's suffering pain. Poor Mum."

"I'm sorry, Andrew." Her eyes filled with tears, like his. "What should I do?"

98

"Let's risk it. It'll only take a minute."

They slipped into the room. Ishbel wanted to cling to him but he shook her off. He bent over his mother and kissed her.

Ishbel through her tears noticed that there was nothing in the room, neither crucifix nor sacred picture, to show that here was a Christian preparing to meet her Maker.

"I've brought Ishbel, Mum."

Ishbel came closer to the bed. Mrs. Niven stared up at the ceiling.

"Andrew said you wanted to hear it out of my own mouth," she said.

Ishbel was puzzled. She turned to Andrew but he shook his head.

"If you're thinking," went on the sick woman, "that whatever you do once I'm gone is nane of my business, then you're wrang. I've loved my son from the minute he was born, and nobody's going to tell me that wherever I am I'll still not love him and wish him well."

"I love him too, Mrs. Niven, and wish him well."

"If that's true then leave him alone. Let him marry one of his ain kind. If he were to marry you the first thing he'd have to throw away would be his pride."

"I wouldn't want to marry a man without pride, Mrs. Niven."

"It wouldn't be your fault. It's your religion. It's been hammered into you from the day you were born. Your kind want everything, down to the souls of weans still unborn."

Ishbel appealed to Andrew. He shook his head, as if to say not to heed his poor mother who so obviously was too ill to know what she was saying. Tears still wetted his cheeks and he was sobbing.

But Ishbel shook her head too. She meant that she could not lie to someone who was probably dying. To her the dead were holy. She prayed for them. She bought candles to ease their torment. She had to respect any promise she made them.

"When your kind get their claws in," muttered Mrs. Niven, "you never let go."

"Has Andrew told you, Mrs. Niven?"

Mrs. Niven waited. "Told me what?"

"That he and I will have to get married."

The sick woman for the first time turned her head and stared at Ishbel. "Are you saying you're expecting a wean?"

"Yes."

"And you're going to hae the papish impudence to say my son's to blame?"

"Andrew is the father, Mrs. Niven. Ask him."

"I shall ask him nothing of the kind. I kent there would be something like this. Was it your mither put you up to it? Or the priest? But I've got my answer ready. If you were going to hae a dozen weans then I'd hae a dozen reasons for saying no."

"He's given me solemn promises, Mrs. Niven."

"And you've given him your —." The word was one of the foulest in the language, though heard often enough in the streets round about.

Ishbel was shocked, all the more so because the accusation, delivered in hate, was partly true. She had forced her body on Andrew. She had turned the Virgin to the wall. She had listened to her mother's whispers.

"Wait for me outside," whispered Andrew, taking her over to the door. "She doesn't really know what she's saying. Never mind. It's us that are concerned, not her. Trust me."

Nodding, she went out; but as she sat and waited, trying to pray, over her prayers kept clouding distrust of him. Why had he not taken her part? Surely his child that was going to be born was as important as his mother who might be going to die.

Perhaps, she thought in terror, he was like his father, and would desert her as callously as his mother had been deserted.

12

THAT SAME SUNDAY, in the afternoon, while Billy was at his Aunt Beatrice's and Andrew somewhere with Ishbel McKenzie, Peggy met Robert Logan by arrangement under the iron shelter at Bridgeton Cross, in the heart of what she called the ghetto. Though there was an underground lavatory beneath his feet Robert looked quite elegant as he waited there, in an almost new dark-blue suit, fawn raincoat, and square-toed shoes. He even had a hat, with a small iridescent feather, but he carried this self-consciously in his hand.

The weather was still cold and wet, and at that time in the afternoon, three o'clock, it was almost dark, though the street lamps were not yet lit.

"Well," said Peggy, appearing suddenly at his side.

He was startled. "Hello, Peggy. I didn't see you coming."

"No. You were miles away. You're a toff."

"Well, Mrs. Bryce wanted me to wear them. I wasn't very keen."

"Why not? You look quite handsome, and I'm sure your feet are dry for a change. There's a stink of moth balls off you, though."

"Yes, I know. But, you see, they've been hanging in a wardrobe for years."

An old man trudged up the iron steps of the urinal, buttoning his fly with hands too cold and shaky to do it properly.

"I hope you're not having to pay too high a price," said Peggy, smiling.

He went sulky.

"I'm sorry. I shouldn't have said that. I'm envious of your

good luck, that's all. You know me: an envious bitch."

"Nobody's less envious," he said, still huffy. Then he suddenly remembered. "Oh, Peggy, I forgot. Your mother. How is she?"

"Dying."

"Dying?"

"That's right."

He wanted to say something that would obliterate the cold sad word, but there was nothing. "I'm sorry, Peggy."

Another old man passed them on his way to the urinal. He did not look pleased at seeing them there. In his view it was no place for courting.

"Was your father there?" asked Robert.

"Where?"

"At the hospital."

"No."

"Maybe he went after you were all gone."

"I thought of that, so I phoned; but he hadn't been."

"It's terrible. I would never have thought your father would have done such a cruel thing."

"Now, Robert, he that's without sin etc. etc." She smiled and patted his arm. "It makes for an interesting world, don't you think? But we're not going to stand here all day, I hope. It's not only moth balls I'm smelling now."

"Will we take a bus?"

"No. Let's walk."

"But you've got nothing to cover your head."

"I can borrow your hat if it gets too wet."

They left the shelter, stood in the rain waiting for a gap in the traffic, and then ran towards the pavement. There, almost immediately, they were accosted by three youths who knew Robert. They were about to swagger into a café but stopped to admire him in his new clothes. They lived in the same tenement as he and had known him all his life. They had left school long ago, to their reiterated blasphemous relief, and regarded him, still at his lessons, as a freak. Usually they were good-natured about it, though filthy-tongued; but sometimes they interpreted too accurately his smile of pity and forgiveness and theatened to belt it off his effing face.

Each of them wore round his neck a Rangers scarf.

Their leader, Chuck McDaid, had a cigarette hanging from his lips. Even in winter he had freckles.

"Well, for Christ's sake," he cried, "if it's no' the cripple-kicker himself, dressed like Anthony Eden. Except for the keeker." He dabbed the bruise under Robert's eye with a tough nicotined finger. "Have you been robbing a pawn shop?"

His henchmen laughed.

"It was time you took a kick at that crabbed old bastard of a faither," went on McDaid. "Good for you, Bobby. Shake." He grabbed Robert's hand and shook it sarcastically. "Shake hands with oor hero, you mugs."

Grinning, his cronies shook Robert's hand in turn.

"You'd bloody well think," leered one of them, "to hear my old man talking that he won the effing war himself. Shagging Italian bints mair like. I've had to cut him doon to size."

"A' these war heroes," said the third, "should stuff their medals up their arses."

"Watch it, Jack," said McDaid. "Don't you see there's a lady present? You're Niven, ain't you? I've seen you around. Live at the top of Minden Street, among the nobs. What the effing hell does that brother of yours think he's up to, going round with that McKenzie judy. She's an effing pape, ain't she?"

"Maybe he's just looking for a free shag, Chuck," grinned Jack. "For a pape she's got nice tits."

"No' even for free shags," said McDaid, earnestly. "If he makes a kid wi' her he's made anither pape, in't he, and there are too effing many of them in this toon as it is. It's been calculated that if they keep on breeding at the rate they're doing they'll ootnumber us Prods in thirty years. For Christ's sake. We'll still be alive to see it."

"There'll hae to be anither Boyne Water," said Jack.

"This is a serious problem," muttered McDaid. "Be seeing you." Then he went into the café, followed by his friends.

Peggy and Robert walked on. He was pale and trembling.

"Sorry, Peggy," he said.

"Why should you apologise? You said nothing."

"That's just it."

"Neither did I."

"They insulted you." He went on angrily, "But you might as well talk to a cageful of tigers."

"I thought you were always full of compassion for them? Victims of the ghetto, and all that."

"You know that's a word I never use. And I wish you wouldn't use it."

"Ghetto?" She began to speak as if reading out of a book. "Let us take a truthful look about us. Mile upon mile of tall grim tenements, greasy pavements, and littered streets. People have been shut up here for generations. They have all kinds of common characteristics. The specimens we have just encountered were of the Protestant variety; they have their Catholic counterparts, who if anything are more bestial."

"Bestial's a terrible word."

"It's a terrible thing."

"There are far more respectable people living here than scum like McDaid."

"You know, given a choice between that sort of respectability and McDaid's bestiality, I'd have to hesitate."

"It's not you that's being bitter, Peggy."

"Who is it then?"

"You're worried about your mother; and about your father too, of course."

"It's still me, isn't it?"

He glanced at her head sodden with rain. "We should take a bus."

"I'm not in as big a hurry to get to Maud as you are. McDaid congratulated you on hitting your father. I wonder what he would have said if you had told him you were sleeping with Maud. I suppose he would have congratulated you again. She's not a Catholic, and she's got bigger breasts than Ishbel McKenzie."

They walked on the whole length of a tenement that stretched for over a hundred yards. Neither spoke. They could hear the rain spitting on the pavement.

"There's such a thing as love, Peggy," he said at last.

"Is there, Robert?"

"You know fine there is."

"Tell me about it."

They were now passing another long tenement, so dilapidated as to be almost a slum. There were dingy little shops in it, the kind that sold cheap sweets, dear groceries on credit, and the more sordid Sunday newspapers. There were some soaked placards. One shouted: "CONFESSIONS OF SOCIETY CALL GIRL"; and another, "RANGERS SHOCK".

"Does it exist here?" she asked.

"Here?"

"Yes, here. The Chuck McDaid country."

"Yes, it does. If any outsider denied it you'd be the first to attack him."

"One lies in support of one's family."

"It wouldn't be lies. You know as well as I do that many of the people who live here are good and kind. Take old

Maggie Ralston as an example. You could get nobody kinder."

"We weren't talking about kindness. We were talking about love."

"Where there's kindness there's bound to be love."

"As Chuck would say, that's a lot of crap."

"No, it isn't. Maybe it's a miracle that love is able to exist here. But it does."

"Keep your miracles. I don't believe in them. You said that worry about my mother was making me bitter."

"I don't blame you."

"All right. I'll be just as magnanimous. I won't blame you either for being made so optimistic by the prospect of having Maud in bed with you tonight. She's quite voluptuous."

"I'm not going to be angry, Peggy. It's yourself you're torturing. You can't bear the disappointment your father has caused you."

"As Chuck would say—"

"You would never admit it, Peggy, but you admired your father."

"He'd be surprised to hear you say that. He thought I thought he was a hypocrite. So he was."

"We all are, in some ways."

"But it's worth it, isn't it, Robert?"

"I used to think of your father as the best type of Glaswegian."

She spoke again as if out of a book. "Born in Culdean Street, in the heart of the ghetto, in a ragstore. Brought up by a humphy-backed aunt who went about the streets blowing a bugle and carrying a bag of rags over her shoulder. Left school at fourteen and worked in a dozen or so odd jobs. Married a factory-girl out of a tenement. Called himself a Protestant but never went to church, or very seldom. Gave his children a better education than he got himself, thus rousing in his neighbours envy and resentment. When war came volunteered, served in the H.L.I., and became a sergeant. Looted a small silver eagle that still sits on the mantelpiece. Afterwards became an insurance collector and rose to be superintendent. Watched his wife grow into a typical fat Glasgow body who preferred playing whist to reading books. Went 'doon the watter' to Rothesay and Millport for family holidays. Liked to poke in rock pools alone. Liked sausage baked in egg for tea. Quoted from books he had never read. Saw his two sons capped at University. Grew old, acquired grandchildren, and was fairly satisfied. And died, still in the ghetto."

"You didn't mention his daughter."

She suddenly stopped. "I'm sorry, Robert. I'm afraid I can't face Maud after all."

"But you'd enjoy talking to her, Peggy. She knows a lot about books."

"Well, that's her job, isn't it? Sorry, Robert. Cheerio."

She turned and began to walk back the way they had come.

Shocked and full of pity at the despair he thought he had seen on her face he hurried after her.

"Where are you going, Peggy?"

She stopped at a bus stop. One of the green and yellow Corporation buses was approaching.

"Let me come with you."

"Maud's waiting for you."

"Will you go home?"

"Eventually."

"I wish I could help you, Peggy."

She said nothing. The bus stopped, she jumped on, and went inside. She did not look back.

A bus going away, down a dreary wintry street, squirting filthy slush from its wheels, was a familiar enough sight in

Glasgow. Yet he stood staring as if he had never seen it before. Sadness and fear mingled in his mind. Everything was strange and ominous. People he loved, like his father and Peggy Niven, surrendered to the ugliness and brutality of life under his very eyes, as if he was the evil influence causing it. Perhaps he was. Tonight like last night and the night before he and Maud would lie together in bed naked on top of the electric blanket, while downstairs the old woman sucked digestive tablets and talked to herself about her slain son.

13

MR. PEFFERMILL WAS amused, but at the same time a
trifle disappointed, not to say intimidated, by his dainty
little Florence's continued virulence against Niven. Knowing
how cordially she had hated the big show-off, and pleased
rather than not by it, as Niven was a man whose pretensions
he had not much cared for himself, he had expected her to
condemn, but he had hardly looked for such vitriolic detesta-
tion. Had it been expressed loudly and vulgarly, in Bess
Niven vein, he would have felt badly let down, for his
Chrissie had accustomed him to modesty and quietness in a
woman, even when in mortal agony. But Florence did it all
as quietly as if she had a sleeping babe at her breast.

However, he had to remonstrate a little, good-humouredly,
when she declared that of all the cruelties perpetrated during
the war, by Nazis, Stalinists, or Japs, none was so vicious as
Niven's forsaking of his stricken wife.

"Now, Florence," he said, laughing and patting her wrist,
"don't spoil your case by exaggerating. Niven used no
physical violence that I've heard of. Did not the Nazis make
millions of Jews, and Jewesses, young and old, fat and thin,
noses hooked or straight, strip off until they were mother
naked and enter gas chambers under the impression these
were baths for cleansing purposes? Did they not afterwards
wrench out all the gold teeth? Were not lampshades made
out of human skin? Now, my dear, you just cannot say that
what Niven did was worse than that."

"I can say it and I do say it. Those Jews were strangers to
the men that slaughtered them like beasts. Niven did it to a

woman who'd lain beside him for more than twenty years, and had borne him three children. She trusted him with more than her life."

He chuckled. "And what could that be, my dear?"

"Her pride as a woman."

"Uh-huh." No feminist, but a fair-minded man, he thought he saw what she meant, though he doubted if many qualified. Big Bess certainly did not: delicacy, in sexual and other matters, was hardly her forte. He could not help remembering with distaste her performance that evening at the whist table. His Chrissie, no paragon, had endured acuter and more prolonged pain with far greater dignity.

"If she dies," said Florence, "he should be hanged."

He tut-tutted sincerely. If not disciplined, women would sabotage the universe, worse than any Communists. Hanging must be reserved for murder and treason. He said so.

"If she dies then he killed her. Would that not be murder?"

"And if she recovers, as we all fervently hope?"

"Then a knife should be used on him."

"I do not quite follow you, my dear."

"I mean he should have done to him what shepherds do to male lambs."

An odd way of putting it, he thought. Shepherds and their lambs were more often looked upon as representing trust and gentleness. Was not Christ frequently portrayed as a shepherd with a lamb in His arms? But of course real shepherds, those who trudged the sodden hills in dubbined boots, for statutory wages, did not use knives; they used their teeth and swallowed the testicles as delicacies.

Still, to prevent a male creature from procreating it was not necessary to slice off the entire fixture; one little cord was all that needed to be cut. Of course there was a rough justice, peculiarly attractive to the female mind, in ensuring that there should never again be pleasure in the act of sex for an adulterer. Better in that case to leave him capable of desire but not of satisfying it. As for adultresses, weren't there tribes in Africa that performed some kind of ritual female circumcision, the purpose of which was to make the physical processes of love-making almost as painful as childbirth, thus discouraging extramarital ploys and, within marriage, leaving the man to get on with it as nature intended?

"A spy that sells his country is no worse," Florence was now saying.

"That again, my dear, is a much bigger statement than you really mean."

"Women that during the war slept with other men while their own were away fighting for king and country were condemned, and rightly so. Compared to Niven's, their sin was slight."

This touched him on a nerve that was very sensitive. Not because Chrissie had ever cuckolded him; he was sure she had not; but because he himself, tempted by foreign whores, had never had the courage to sample them.

He adopted his elder's tone. "Surely, Florence, such women were far more despicable than Niven? Their husbands were daily in danger of death, as you should know. Who better? But for the sure knowledge that their wives were being faithful to them they could not in many cases have endured it."

"That's true, but remember this, those men were far away and didn't see their wives lying with other men."

"I was not aware that Niven had committed adultery under Bess's nose."

"He as good as did. You heard him tell her, as she lay helpless with pain, that he had a fancy woman."

"I do not recall his using those actual words."

"It came to the same thing."

"You may be right. But did she not forgive him on the spot? I heard her myself."

Florence could say nothing to that. He knew why. She thought forgiveness almost as unforgivable as the wrong it forgave. "Well, anyway, my dear," he said, soothingly, "although Bess is our good friend there is really nothing we can do at present to help her."

"We could notify his employers and get him sacked."

"You are jumping to conclusions. They might consider his private life no concern of theirs. For principle's sake I might be inclined to take that view myself."

"It's different where money's concerned."

"Ah, you mean they might be afraid he will embezzle in order to keep his paramour happy? That is not improbable, though I doubt if Niven is ever in a position to lay his hands on any considerable sum. But there is another aspect to be considered. I have heard you say yourself he must not be allowed to escape from his financial obligations to his family. Agreed. But would it not be helping him to escape from those obligations if we had him dismissed?"

"She's got money."

"She?"

"His fancy woman."

"But this is pure supposition, my dear."

"It's commonsense. Do you think he'd go off with somebody as poor as himself? He's conceited to the last hair in his moustache."

But Mr. Peffermill was losing interest in the conversation. Why should he waste time, thought, and opportunity, on people like the Nivens? He had his own love life to talk about and promote.

They were in his flat, prior to setting out for the evening service. He had hoped—no, hoped was too strong a word, toyed with the fancy was better—he had toyed with the fancy that he might get her into bed or at least on to the sofa. At the moment they were sitting on adjacent easy chairs in front of the fire, so close together that he could easily reach forward and pat her hand.

"Enough of the Nivens for the time being, my dear. Let's think of ourselves for a change."

He saw her lips tighten. This was a danger signal that Bess Niven curiously enough had warned him about. "When Flo tightens her lips, Peffy, it's time to smack her bottom."

Or fondle it. Taking her ever so gently by the hand he allowed himself ten seconds or so to increase his grip with gradual accesses of affection. Then he began to pull. At first it was more a firm caress than a summons. But slowly the tug became more imperious. If she had remained in her own chair her arm would have been quite strained, and for a few moments it looked as if she would prefer dislocation, but suddenly with a smile that ended the rebellion on her mouth, she came up and over and on to his blue serge knees, as gracefully as if it was part of a dance. In everything she did she was so dainty. Himself far from laborious, their love-making was sure to be as elegant as that of butterflies on the wing; but of course with rather more impact.

Her eyes policed his hands so that these had to give up for the moment their skulking movements and settle on the arms of his chair. She perched on rather than nestled in his lap. Her own hands, as an example to his, were clasped most unlasciviously at her navel, as if in prayer. Kissing her would have been pointless since, without a good grip, he could have exerted no force of passion. On the contrary he might have dislocated his own neck or sent her sliding to the floor. What made his abstinence less tolerable was her evident approval of it. Indeed, after two or three minutes of this abortive dandling he began to suspect her mind was not on him at all, on no part of him, seen or unseen.

No, by St. Augustine, it was still on Niven.

"When somebody's been sentenced to be hanged for murder," she said, "you know how some fools get up a petition to have him reprieved. They pester you in the street to sign. I am proud to say I have never signed one in my life."

Neither had he. But he refused to say so, not out of shame, but out of indignation that she should choose in such circumstances to bring up so ghoulish a subject.

"Often I've felt," she went, "like getting up another petition, to be signed by all those who thought he should be hanged, and the higher the better."

"The height is scientifically measured," he said coldly. "Higher would not mean better."

"More people would see him."

"How could it mean that, my dear?" he demanded. "You know, or ought to know, that hangings are no longer public."

"They should be. Well, I'm thinking of getting up a petition against Niven."

"Good God, how could you do that?"

"Oh, there would be nothing to sign. I would just go round all the people who knew him and get them to say to my face what a black-hearted villain they think he is."

His fingers, wishing it was her thigh, dug into the arms of his chair. "Take care," he cried. "You might get some surprises. Opinions often turn out to be strange things when they're forced out into the light."

"Surely there wouldn't be a single one would justify him?"

He saw the necessity of there being not only one but a certain few. It was impossible to explain it to her, not because she hated Niven too much but simply because she was a woman. Life was not a clean, tidy, well-run, well-furnished house. Society and civilised behaviour, which prevented him for instance from raping her there and then, were founded on brute force; which had meant in the recent war the butchery of millions, and, now he came to think of it, the rape of thousands.

"You're not in earnest about this, Florence?"

"Why shouldn't I be? It's the least I can do for Bess."

"But she's the very woman who would forbid you. Has she not forgiven him? Does she not want him back?"

"Poor soul, she's in no state of mind to know what she wants."

"I'm afraid, Florence, I'll have to think this over."

"But I'm asking you to do nothing, Ben. I'll do all the petitioning myself."

"By George, Florence, you're asking me to do a great deal. You're asking me to approve of my wife-to-be going round this neighbourhood where I'm known and highly respected, talking about a case that, God knows how, has been kept out of the newspapers so far, but which is liable to appear in them any day. I ought to warn you, my dear, that above all else I dislike notoriety in a woman."

She was silent, but rather perversely her face began to lose its bitter lines and become sweeter than he had ever seen it before.

"I was never notorious," she murmured.

It was tantamount to some kind of invitation. One of those too ready law-breakers, his hands, came louping off the arm of the chair on to her thigh.

"Bless you, my darling," he said hoarsely. "Of course you never were."

His other hand, the weaker left, remained where it was, twitching; but it wasn't needed so far, the right had got enough purchase now to enable him to bring their faces close enough for a worth-while kiss. He had heard of sour-mouthed hard-hurdied women, past their prime, who gave out love as a tree did rubber, in slow sticky drops. That kiss proved his Florence was not one of them. She flung her arms round his neck and kissed him warmly back. He was ravished, in spite of a suspicion that she might be thus bestowing on him this second-class privilege of a betrothed not wholly out of affection; that she was in fact hoping to wheedle out of him permission for that absurd petition against Niven. Well, there was nothing to prevent him raising the price. Into her small, neat, clean, fresh-smelling ear he whispered a proposal itself clean enough and quite inoffensively worded.

"That's for later," she said, "after the wedding."

Well, it had happened to Napoleon too; who had been told the road to bed lay through the church. Feeling imperialistic, he whispered that a man in love kept waiting for the fruits thereof was apt to uproot the whole tree in his frenzy. As he spoke his hand was voyaging well up her thigh, inside her skirt.

She stopped it, with a small hand that had a grip like a monkey wrench.

"We'll see," she said enigmatically. Then she added, "Your name's at the top of the list, isn't it?"

He reflected. Yes, why not? Only Niven's reputation would be made to stink, as it deserved.

"Very well." He took his reward, another kiss and squeeze.

After all, big Niven ought to have waited until death released him, as Ebenezer Peffermill had had to do.

"Still, my dear, mind what I said. Not everyone will sign it."

"Those that don't will give themselves away. They'll show what's in their hearts. Now don't you think it's about time we made ourselves respectable for church?"

All he needed to do was take down his black overcoat and pale grey hat from the hallstand. He said so.

She tweaked his cheek. "I meant, in our minds," she whispered, leaving him to wonder what lewdness had been in hers, and also whether, if he had persevered, he could after all have outdone Napoleon and coaxed her into half an hour of pre-marital bed.

14

THAT VERY EVENING Flo collected quite a number of invisible signatures at the church. Bess, though not all that regular a worshipper, was well-liked there, being as jolly in her devotions as at whist. Therefore everyone Flo approached agreed at once Niven had behaved abominably. Some did not wait to be asked. Hearing what Flo was about they came and volunteered their opinion that though the Lord could no doubt in His own good time be trusted to punish such wickedness as it deserved, still there ought to be a way for Niven to be given a foretaste here on earth: flogging with the cat-o'-nine-tails was suggested by one grim lady who offered to wield it herself.

Mr. Peffermill, in the background, was amused but alarmed too by this evidence of primitive savagery in these respectable Christian matrons.

Mr. Brewster, the minister, was at present at loggerheads with a majority of his congregation who thought him much too mild in his preaching. He made their Christ out to be a glaikit softie who would let the whole world spit on Him.

Flo boldly sought him out in the vestry after the service. A tall sour-looking man, he still had on his gown, liking, so he said, rudely, to sit in uninterrupted meditation for at least half an hour.

"After divine communion, however imperfect," he said, "it's difficult to bring back one's mind to ordinary affairs."

What he was telling her of course was to go to hell and not bother him. She was furious.

"This is no ordinary affair," she said, and explained what it was.

"Yes, I've heard about it," he said, sourer than ever. "At first I just couldn't believe it. Mungo Niven always struck me as a superior sort of person."

"Superior?" She turned pale.

"He seemed to me to be always searching for something better."

"Well, he seems to have found her."

"I was referring to spiritual qualities, Mrs. McTaggart."

"He seldom troubled your church, Mr. Brewster, with his spiritual qualities."

The minister sneered. "It's not for me to say that deprivation of my sermons lessens a man's worth."

"If it isn't for you to say, who is it for then? Pardon my frankness, Mr. Brewster, but if you think your sermons are all that unimportant, why give them? Superior, you said. Superior in what? I would like to know."

Mr. Brewster in the past year had tried for three other charges. He knew that in the faction opposed to him Mrs. McTaggart was an energetic member. This intrusion into the vestry was apparently some kind of test. Outside in the empty church no doubt sly little treacherous Peffermill waited to hear her report, which would soon be spread among the disaffected.

If it was not much of a martyrdom that was simply because the souls of the persecutors were so puny.

The minister stared down at his hands resting on the table. He moved one a little so that both together represented roughly the map of Scotland. Where his right thumb was lay Innellan, a charge that carried a stipend nearly four hundred pounds above the minimum; but that was not the reason why he had applied. Similarly with Elgin, lying somewhere near the knuckle of his left forefinger. Perhaps what he was seeking did not exist: a pulpit surrounded by friends and well-wishers, who would encourage him in his heavy and holy task, the explaining of Christ, Exemplar of Love, to man, Craver of Love. In his present church, deep in tenement land, he was preaching to hearts as stony as the cobbles in the streets.

"Superior?" he repeated. "A man can commit a great sin because there is greatness in his soul."

"So now it's greatness? How can you, a minister of God, dressed in your robes, use such words about a man who saw his wife of twenty-five years lying in agony and jumped on her with both his feet? A superior jumper, did you mean? Great at cruelty?"

"I appreciate your feelings, Mrs. McTaggart. I know that you and Mrs. Niven were close friends."

He thought about Mrs. Niven. Hearty, good-humoured, and vulgar, she was as vindictively prejudiced against Catholics as anyone in this bigoted city. He had once remarked, casually, for it was so obvious, that many Catholics were better Christians than some Protestants. She had stiffened with rage and affront. Remembering the incident, he felt stubborn about wholeheartedly condemning her husband, especially as this friend of hers, Mrs. McTaggart, was waiting for that condemnation like one of the ghouls who used to wait at the foot of the scaffold for relics of some holy man murdered for his faith.

"Who can see beneath the surface?" he asked. "Who is so pure as to be a judge?"

"Thou shalt not commit adultery, Mr. Brewster."

She made it sound not so much a quotation as an admonition. Like the rest she knew, or suspected, that his relations with his own wife were not harmonious.

"There is always repentance, Mrs. McTaggart. It may be

that Niven will show his superiority by the quality of his repentance."

"You'll have to explain that to me, Mr. Brewster. I'm a simple woman."

"Some men who desert their wives never afterwards waste a thought on them. I do not think Niven is one of those. He will suffer much remorse."

"As soon as his fancy woman gets tired of him, yes; but not before."

He was handicapped as a disciple of Christ, Exemplar of Love, by having to try so hard not to hate this small, neat, quiet woman so representative of everything that made his sacred task next to impossible.

About to play his trump card he tried to keep spite out of his voice. As drably as he could he said, "I visited Mrs. Niven in hospital this afternoon."

She was taken aback. "I understand only her closest kin were being allowed in. But I forgot: you have privileges."

"Not I, but Christ in me."

She sniffed.

"It was Mrs. Niven who used the word you find so objectionable."

"Superior?"

"Yes, superior."

"So she's still blind?"

"Do not say that, Mrs. McTaggart. That poor sick woman said, very proudly, 'My Mungo was always a superior sort of man, Mr. Brewster.' I confess I was astonished at first. In the circumstances it wasn't the word that would have sprung to my mind."

"Nor to mine, in any circumstances."

"She begged me to do what I can to get him to return to her. I was greatly moved. Forgiveness is always magnificent."

"It's your job to say so," she said, rising and going out,

determined never to step inside that church again as long as he was its minister.

During the week that followed she went about amassing support for the condemnation of Niven. Mostly she got it straight away, without any trouble; but these too often were people whose opinions upon any other subject she would never have bothered asking and those approval gave her no satisfaction. Others approved only after some sharp prodding; this was not because they were reluctant to condemn Niven but because they did not like to commit themselves to anything.

As Ben had prophesied there were a few who refused their support.

Big Aird, the engine-driver, was one. Catching sight of him in McPherson's the tobacconist, she went in out of the cold to talk to him there. He listened and then said, "You mind what wee Peffermill said that night Bess took bad, aboot women being the sources o' life? Well, maybe you were wi' Bess in the ladies' when he said it, but he did say it. It's occurred to me often since, shunting up and doon, to wonder just how many sources o' life there are. Maybe big Niven's gone off in search o' some o' them that aren't to be found hereaboots. I've always liked Bess, so I'm no' saying good luck to him, but I'm no' saying hell mend him either."

It was true then what they said about him: that if he had had any brains he would have got a job years ago driving passenger trains instead of wagon loads of coal and dross.

Oh yes, those few withholders of their signatures were sorry for Bess, but it was clear enough they also admired Niven and envied him.

She went to see Carmichael, notorious socialist and councillor for the district. Though she would sooner have voted

121

for a dog than for him, still in the past she had granted him some respect for speaking his mind once to visiting royalty, on the subject of war pensions. Besides, he was known to be honest about such things as council house waiting lists.

Small and squat, with a face like a boozy boxer, he was at least not conceited about his appearance like Niven.

He listened with professional attentiveness as she urged that it was his duty to denounce Niven publicly at the next ward meeting. He let her speak herself out, and kept waiting when she had nothing more to say. No one had ever used such tactics on her before. It was a pity she could not truthfully tell herself there was a smell of drink off his breath. It must be stupidity.

"You're forgetting something, woman," he said at last, in his rough aggressive Glasgow voice. "I'm the keeper of nae man's conscience."

"Is that so, Mr. Carmichael? Then let me tell you I've heard you say some very blistering things about the consciences of Tories who, according to you, were callous about old-age pensioners and the like."

"Callous in their public capacity," he said. "I ken Tories wha are mair charitable in private than lots of Socialists."

"It's big of you to admit it."

"It's honest of me to admit it. I've heard about Niven, and I'm sorry it's happened. It's never a pleasure to hear of a marriage that's broken up after twenty-five years. I'm saying that as a private individual. As a councillor I hae no right to speak on such a matter."

"What about the money aspect, Mr. Carmichael? He's left them withoot a penny. There's a boy at University."

"If I can help there I'll be pleased to. Ask the lad to come and see me."

"So you'd let Niven put his family on the public assistance?"

"You're letting dislike run awa' wi' you, woman. Take care it doesnae drap you at the feet of the deil."

She gasped at that: she, a kirk-goer, threatened by a known atheist.

"You're talking as if you'd like the stocks brought back again. You'd like to see Niven bound hand and foot in George Square, so that every hooligan could throw rotten tomatoes at him."

"Not only hooligans, Mr. Carmichael; and it wouldn't be tomatoes I'd throw. It'd be stones."

She rose. "For a man with the experience you brag about you seemed to have missed the simple truth."

"Often the truth's not so simple."

"It is, councillor, always. Only some so-called clever folk don't like to recognise it as such. Otherwise, who would call them clever? In this present case, the simple truth is that Niven, having got all the pleasure he could out of his wife's body, went away and found another more to his taste. That's the simple truth for you. Good evening."

She could never be sure afterwards, but it seemed to her that as she went out he muttered, "Pleasure, for Christ's sake?" And out on the street, putting up her umbrella, she smiled with some satisfaction. For she had temporarily forgotten that Carmichael's own wife was said to have a temper like a drunken whore's.

Of course, she thought, in a sudden revelation, every man that defends Niven or refuses to condemn him is really admitting that he too would like to run away from his wife. There was the minister, with a whiner to look after his manse and warm his bed; Aird, with hairy-chinned Jean; and now Carmichael.

It was a relief to talk to Nan Fraser who, living up the same close, and being a bonny fresh young woman, was in a

123

better position than most to judge Niven. Hadn't there been rumours once that *she* was his fancy woman?

"To tell you the truth, Mrs. McTaggart," she whispered, too modest to say it loudly, "there were times when I was frightened and ashamed just to talk to him here in the street or in the close, in passing."

"And why that, Nan?"

"He looked at me as if—I blush to say it—as if I had no clothes on. You're the first I've ever mentioned it to, I felt so ashamed. If I had told my Alec heaven knows what he would have done."

Neither remarked that Niven was six inches taller and three stones heavier than her Alec.

"I know exactly what you mean, Nan. I warned Bess many a time."

Nan closed her eyes. "I used to lie in bed at night and worry about Peggy. I mean, a man with a look like that in his eyes could be capable of anything; even with his own daughter."

"Exactly."

"Maybe it was as well poor Peggy's so thin and, well, not what you would call attractive. In a way it's a blessing he's gone. In the long run Bess will be better off without him. That's to say if the poor soul ever comes out of hospital alive. You know, Mrs. McTaggart, there are people who think he's handsome and superior."

"Fools!"

"Honestly, I could never see it myself." Nan giggled. "Maybe because I've always had a prejudice against men with moustaches."

Archie McTaggart, killed in Africa, had had a moustache. But allies ought not to fall out.

"The main thing is," said Mrs. McTaggart, "the best of us saw through him."

"Where do you think he is, Mrs. McTaggart? He once told me he had a hankering to live in a country where the sun shone every day."

"Well, if he's gone there it's certainly not with his money. He's got some admirers, as you've said, Nan. What would they say if they heard he was off to Spain or Italy using his fancy woman's money?"

Nan nodded, thrilled more than shocked by this addition to Niven's wickedness.

The worst insult was to come from somebody so worthless that Flo would never have thought of seeking her adherence. This was Maggie Ralston, that giggling grey-haired imbecile. Flo met her by accident in the co-operative grocer's, shuffling her swollen feet in the sawdust because, as she explained in her squelchy little voice, she'd tramped on dog's dirt on the pavement.

That was Flo's cue. "There's worse than dog's dirt," she said.

Maggie nodded. "Human's worse."

"I meant what can't be touched or seen or smelled."

"Is this a riddle, Flo?" She giggled.

"I'm not joking."

"No, the woman that made the jokes is no' fit to make them any longer. Poor Bess. Whit's the latest news? I was talking to young Peggy yesterday. It seems they're no' sure whether this operation's been a success or no.'"

"Which means it hasn't."

"You think they'll bring her hame to dee?"

"That's what they usually do."

Maggie sighed, and lifted one bauchle of a foot to rub it against the other. Her neck was not clean. Her raincoat stank of turpentine or paraffin. On her head she had a dustcap of grey plastic, decorated with tiny prancing cats, each with a red bow round its neck and its tail up.

"I'm going to let you into a secret, Flo. There are times when I get fair scunnered myself at a' this rain and cauld and grey skies. Even the mice in your hoose are miserable."

"There are no mice in my house, thank you."

Maggie smiled. "There wouldnae be, Flo. Whit I meant was this. Big Mungo Niven, God forgie him, once said to me, 'Maggie, there are places where the skies are always blue and where even a half-starved dog finds life bearable.' I'll never forget the look on his face when he said that. So I just cannae bring myself to condemn him, Flo, though it was a terrible thing he did. A mair terrible thing must hae driven him to it."

"Filthy lust, you mean."

Maggie smiled again. "That reminds me, Flo: when are you and wee Ben Peffermill getting spliced?"

Flo walked away.

15

THE DAY BEFORE leaving for Spain Mungo at ten minutes to four was standing in a closemouth opposite River-bank Senior Secondary School. He hoped to catch Peggy when the school came out.

It was dry, but cold and dull. Two boys came through the pend leading from the playground, one a cripple no doubt given permission to leave before the stampede began. They were dressed in raincoats and thick woollen scarfs. Once out of the gate they went up the street, past the chalked accusations on the wall which said that Big McNaught was a cunt. Shocked, Mungo remembered that this was Billy's English teacher and often had him frightened.

He watched the cripple proceed arduously but blithely, escorted by his friend who must have been released early for that purpose. That, thought Mungo, was the kind of job he would have been given when a boy. Big Mungo, taller and stronger than most, but simpler too, or so it was thought; too good-natured to punish the teasing by smaller boys even when it was malicious and in concert; given tasks of kindness because he was too conscientious to object. He had won no prizes, but one teacher, grey-haired Miss Munn, long since dead, had once whispered to him: "Never mind, Mungo, a good heart is its own reward."

The bell rang. The classes must have been lined up ready to dash out, for within seconds they were streaming out of the two archways, one for boys and the other for girls. Down the steps of the staff entrance in the middle hurried three men teachers carrying brief-cases. For a few moments Mungo imagined himself as one of them, a teacher of history, which had been his favourite subject. If he had had the brains, the money, and the luck to go to University and take a degree, it was very unlikely he would ever have met Bess, who had worked in a carpet factory. He would have married a graduate like himself, so that their children would have had a good chance in life, from the point of view both of financial support and inherited intelligence. Then he realised the thought was disloyal to his actual children who were surely as good and clever as he could wish. But was that quite true? Andrew was shifty and ungrateful; Billy, even at twelve, calculating and selfish; and Peggy was too just, too neutral.

He thought: is this me finding fault with my own children after what I've done to them? If they have faults consider the examples I have shown them.

With far better cause they were no doubt finding fault with him. Their mother too was in hospital seriously ill. Thus the family was breaking up.

"If you see them, Mungo," Myra had said, smiling, "aren't you afraid you might not come back to me? Don't worry. I can always get a refund on that air-ticket, you know."

Then he caught sight of Billy, one of a noisy group throwing to one another the cap of a small boy who dashed to and fro, snivelling and becoming more and more excited. The cap came to Billy. He clapped it on his head, on top of his own cap, and strutted about, making his pals laugh. Mungo was amazed. He had never thought of his son as a bully or humorist. When the boy pleaded for his cap Billy dangled it in front of him, tickled his nose with it, avoided his grabbing hands, and then slapped it on his head, with its peak down over his eyes. The rest cheered. The victim pulled off his cap, examined it, dusted it, put it on, and then trotted off home where he would arrive as bold as any, never letting his mother know about his humiliation.

Peggy came out talking to Robert Logan. Somehow they did not seem as friendly as before. After chatting for two or three minutes outside the gate they separated, Robert going slowly up the street, with several glances back, and Peggy quickly down it, with never a backward glance.

This was strange. Even if Robert was still staying with Maggie Ralston, or had gone back to his parents, his direction was the same as Peggy's. But wherever he was going now it was convenient for Mungo who wanted to speak to Peggy in private.

Crossing the road he hurried after her. It was one of the most anxious moments of his life when he reached forward and said, "Well, Peggy." Returning from her thoughts she recognised him. He must have been expecting her to walk on for when she stopped he felt relief and gratitude.

It was already almost dark. Rain was in the air.

"I want to talk to you, Peggy. Where can we go?"

"There's a café along here."

"Let's go there then and have a cup of coffee."

"At this time it's crammed with kids playing the juke-box."

"It won't do then, will it?"

After their coca-colas and music those kids would go home, where their mothers would be getting tea ready and their fathers would return about five-thirty. But why in Christ's name remember with envy and sentimental regret a domesticity that for years had suffocated him? Not even for his children's sakes would he go back to it.

"Let's walk a bit," he said. "I'll carry your bag."

"No, it's all right."

He made to take it but she would not let him.

"Don't treat me as your enemy, girl," he said bitterly.

She did not answer.

Side by side they walked along the street.

"I've been phoning every day to hear how your mother is," he said. "The operation doesn't seem to have been very successful."

"Three months, Dr. Yellowlees said."

"What do you mean, three months?"

"That's all they expect her to live."

"Why did the old fool say such a thing like that to you, just a schoolgirl."

"There was nobody else to say it to. Anyway, I asked him."

"What about Andrew? He's old enough to take on some responsibility."

"He's doing his best, I suppose."

"When are they bringing her home?"

"In two or three weeks, when she's a bit stronger."

"Aye." He felt baffled, at one moment furious enough to want to crash his fist through one of the lighted shop windows, and the next so ashamed he wanted to fall down on his knees.

He took refuge in what he thought was a safe subject. "I saw you with Robert Logan. So he isn't staying with you?"

"No."

"I noticed he went up Springfield Road. Where was he going?"

"He's staying in Carmyle."

"Carmyle? I didn't know he had any relatives living out there."

"He hasn't. A Miss Bryce has taken him in."

"Who's she?"

"A librarian at our branch. You may have noticed her. Buxom, with reddish hair."

"Huffy-faced woman?" Had he been speaking to another man his description would have been different. He remembered Miss Bryce's fine breasts.

"Sort of, yes."

"Why has she taken him in?"

"He says out of Christian charity."

"Does she live alone?"

"As good as. Her mother's old and arthritic; she sleeps downstairs all the time. So it's convenient for Robert and Maud."

"Maud?"

"That's her name."

"How do you mean convenient?"

"They sleep together."

"My God, Peggy, what are you saying?"

"It isn't all that uncommon. At any rate not in books; and she's a librarian."

"This isn't a joke, Peggy. Does the headmaster know?" It was a silly question. "Does anybody know besides you?"

"Not that I know of."

"This Miss Bryce, she must be about forty."

"About that, yes."

"And he's only eighteen. So, Peggy, this is your paragon who wouldn't even swear."

"He still doesn't swear."

"Somebody should stop it."

"Who?"

"His people. The authorities, the police."

"Isn't sixteen the age of consent in Scotland, for boys as well as girls?"

"Surely you don't approve of this, Peggy?"

"There are other things I don't suppose I approve of either. Nobody asks for my approval. Why should they?"

He knew what she was hinting. He had wanted to invoke authorities in Robert's case. What authorities had been invoked in his own?

"Are you still associating with him?"

"Of course."

"Of course nothing. You shouldn't."

"He's my friend."

"If what you say's true he's a depraved young scoundrel. If she knew your mother would certainly not allow you to have anything to do with him."

"I don't suppose she would."

They had stopped at a windy corner, near a pillar box.

"I'd better get back home," she said. "Billy doesn't like to be left alone in the house after dark."

"Yes, neither he does. What about your cough?"

"It's almost better."

"Shouldn't Andrew be home by this time?"

"He stays at the University longer now. He says he can't concentrate at home."

"That girl, Ishbel McKenzie, is he still going with her?"

She hesitated.

"Well, is he?"

"I suppose so, but I don't really know. She says she's pregnant."

"By Andrew? I mean, does she accuse him?"

"Yes."

"What does he say?"

"He just grins."

"What do you think, Peggy?"

"I don't know."

"What does your mother say?"

"The same as always. She wants him to have nothing to do with her."

"But if he is responsible he ought to marry the girl. Don't you think so, Peggy?"

"I don't know."

"Is that all you can say? You don't know."

"I'm just learning to form judgments. I need more practice."

"You seem to be getting plenty. First, Robert Logan and this woman; and now Andrew. Aye, and me. Did you get the letter, about the money?"

"From the lawyer? Yes."

It had said that the sum of twenty pounds would be sent to them every week. Andrew had been much relieved. The uncles and aunts were divided about accepting. Aunt Beatrice thought not a filthy penny of it should be touched.

"Is it all right, Peggy?"

"About the money, you mean?"

"Yes. It should be enough."

"Andrew seems pleased."

"You don't, though."

She did not answer.

"You see, Peggy, I'm going away. Tomorrow. Out of the country."

She offered no comment.

"To Barcelona, as a matter of fact. The address is on this card."

"They're all Catholics there."

"Most of them anyway. Write to me, Peggy."

"What about?"

"What do you mean, what about?"

"You're not interested in Mum any more, are you? She's all I'll be thinking about for the next three months."

"So you've condemned me, Peggy?"

"If Mum dies," she said, deliberately, "I'll miss her, more than I've ever missed anybody or anything. But what will be harder to bear will be to see Billy missing her."

"Even if I went back I still couldn't save her."

"She said we'd to try and find you. We'd to tell you she wants you to come back to her."

"That's impossible."

"I'm leaving school on Friday."

"Do you mean, to look after your mother?"

"No. For good."

"What are you talking about, Peggy?"

"I've got a job in the steelwork office. Mr. Peffermill got it for me."

"Through that interfering little bitch McTaggart?" He could have wept. This then was her way of punishing him. She knew how proud he was of her cleverness, and how keen that she should go to University.

"Are you doing this to punish me, Peggy?"

"I'm doing it because I'll need money."

"But it's been explained about money."

"I prefer to keep myself."

"No, I can't accept this, Peggy. It would haunt me all my life if I thought I'd ruined your career. What does your headmaster say?"

"He says it's a pity, but he understands."

"Does he? He wouldn't take it so calmly if it was his own girl throwing away a brilliant career."

"I'm not throwing anything away."

"Does your mother know?"

"Not yet."

"This will be meat and drink to your uncles and aunts."

"It's got nothing to do with them. Look, it's almost pitch dark now. Billy will be very anxious. He misses Mum, you know. Especially in the house, at night. I must go."

"You must go. Is that all you've got to say?"

She shrugged her shoulders as if to ask what else could there be to say. Of course there could be nothing.

"I'm sorry," he muttered. "I had no right to speak to you like that. I'm sorry."

"We're all sorry. Goodbye."

"Goodbye, Peggy. Please write."

She did not once look back.

PART TWO

BY THE TIME Andrew's letter arrived, seven weeks after
their arrival in Barcelona, the affair was over. Mungo had
been installed in a bedroom of his own, breakfast was eaten
together, respect was pretended, endearments were omitted,
money was seldom mentioned though often thought about,
acquaintances were told the little they needed to know, and
the ultimate disruption was waited for, as if predestined. It
was a very Scotch dissolution to a very Scotch affair.

For Myra it was simple. Here in this huge cosmopolitan
city, with her friend Ethne McGilvray to launch her, she had
soon met more interesting men. Having served his purpose
Mungo was now totally dispensable.

As for Mungo, financially a prisoner and humiliated daily
by his jailer's increasing meanness, he would have become
quite stunted in the prodigal sunshine had it not been for
Ethne's warm admiration. That she had designs was obvious.
Under the impression that he was at least as well-off as Myra
she kept joking that she and Mungo ought to go off together
on a world cruise. She stuck travel brochures into his pockets.
Nearly forty, with her fair-haired voluptuousness almost gone
to fat, scraping a living by teaching English, with an inter-
lude now and then of being someone's mistress, she had
become desperate.

Myra was neither deceived nor offended. On the contrary,
with a procuress's smile, she would whisper, "You're a god-
send to her, Mungo. Pity you don't have the money she
thinks you have."

This was the situation when the letter arrived. At first,

holding it in his hand, with the Glasgow postmark distinct and Andrew's handwriting recognisable, Mungo did not know whether to be relieved or apprehensive. Peggy had said she would write only if her mother died; but perhaps she had changed her mind even about that, and though her mother was now dead had refused to let him know, carrying her neutrality to the bittermost end. Therefore Andrew, as the eldest, had taken it upon himself to write.

Myra was amused. "You're like those monkeys at the Zoo. You've done everything but chew it."

"It's from Andrew."

"So you've said, twice."

"I'm just wondering what he's got to write about."

"Read it and find out."

"Maybe she's gone."

"Dead, you mean?"

"Aye."

She hoped not. As a widower he might become a nuisance hard to shake off.

"Surely they'd have sent a telegram in that case?"

"Am I worth a telegram?"

"Mungo, this is as good a time as any for a talk I've been intending to have with you. When are you going back? You will have to eventually, so the sooner the better."

"I'm never going back."

"Oh yes, you are, with your lip trembling, as they say in Glasgow. You remembered we agreed that if one or other of us got tired of the relationship he or she was at complete liberty to end it. Be honest, Mungo. Don't you find me tiresome?"

"It's the other way round."

"Let's say it's reciprocal. All the more reason for ending it, as quickly and painlessly as possible. It's time for you to make a move, Mungo. But read your letter. There may be something in it with a bearing on what I'm saying."

He gazed at the envelope in his hand. He remembered the drawer in which the ink was kept. That drawer, in the kitchen dresser, was at all times crammed to overflowing with the oddities that accrued in a family: Bess's old slack garters, Billy's marbles, Andrew's bow-ties, Peggy's ball-point pens. He remembered too Andrew's pen, an expensive Parker, red, bought for his twenty-first birthday. He pictured Andrew's big, grasping hand holding it.

Suddenly this letter represented all his human wealth. Without it here in this flat, in this large foreign city, he was a stranger and a beggar. If it had been from Peggy, in sorrow for her mother, but also in forgiveness and love, he might even have been inspired by it into recovering enough pride and manliness to return home and as a father make up for his failure as a husband.

At last he opened the envelope. There were two sheets of notepaper, lined, because Bess had not liked to write on plain paper, and, as she had frequently pointed out, it was her who did the family shopping.

"Dear Dad,

Only the other day I discovered by accident that Peggy had your address. Knowing our Peg, you can understand what a job I had getting it out of her.

All things considered, Dad, I thought you had a right to know how things stand with us at the moment. Financially, thanks to you, we're fine. Mum, though, isn't very well. She's been home from hospital about four weeks. She's greatly shrunk, I'm sorry to say, and has lost lots of her confidence.

Peggy's working in the steelworks office. She left school, you know. Mr. Peffermill, Flo's beau, got her the job. More mysterious than ever she tells us nothing. Billy plods on at school, still terrified of Belter. Yours truly is slaving away. My finals in June are going to be 'nae bother'.

There's one thing, Dad. Four of my Varsity pals are going to the Continent this Easter. One of them's got the use of his dad's car. Don't worry, they're not likely to get the length of Spain. But they want me to go with them. You'll admit travel's an important part of education nowadays. Fifteen quid would do it. But where am I to get fifteen quid? I don't want to bother Mum. If you could help I'd be much obliged, and, as I think I've said before, I'd take the male view every time. They aren't all Desdemonas. You've only got one life. That's the sum and substance of it, as old Mrs. Gallie used to say. By the way she's gone at last. Guess what, too? Our Peg insisted on taking old Knox in. The rest of us objected because you know how he stinks. How Mum in the old days would have created. Not that he's in the house much. He prefers to sit outside old Hannah's door, much to the annoyance of the new tenants who keep falling over him.

Best wishes. I'm keeping my fingers crossed."

As he read it, over and over again, Mungo grew calmer and more at ease. He wished to blame no-one, not even himself. In some of the old paintings in the Montjuich Museum were scenes of sombre contemplative savagery, men and women being tortured in every way conceivable to fertile minds. Standing in front of that centuries-old vision of the human situation he had somehow not felt outraged or ashamed or even hostile to the dedicated torturers. Nor did he now, holding in his hand this letter that revealed his son's so human selfishness and venality.

"Well?" asked Myra.

She too must be included in his amnesty.

"What does he say?"

He held out the letter, as if it was the answer to all questions.

"Is she dead?"

"No, not that."

"Thank God." She made no effort to disguise the nature of her gratitude. "Is it an appeal for you to go back? Very timely."

"It's not that kind of appeal."

She took the letter but did not yet read it. "I've always been a bit surprised, Mungo, that none of your children took your part; wrote to you at least."

"I was the deserter. Why should they write to me?"

She was amused. "So you were. Well, let's see what the boy has to say." As she read she began to smile. "But, Mungo, he's on your side surely."

"I want nobody to be on my side."

"Poor Mungo, all alone in the world. Well, your Andrew sounds as if he has enough gumption to do well for himself. So we're not all Desdemonas?" She laughed. "I'm sure you subscribe to that. You know, I'm inclined to think a remark like that's worth fifteen pounds."

"You want to corrupt him further?"

"I want to give him a chance to learn more about the world he lives in, and he'll never do that if he stays in Scotland all his days. There he'll be satisfied with the three-room and kitchen and tiled close that contented your generation."

"If it had contented me would I be here?"

"Here, Mungo, but so lost, so guilty-looking. Betrayed by whole generations of kettle-on-the-hob rectitude. Mungo, with you it's necessary to be brutal at times. Here it is then. Agree to return to Scotland within a week and I'll not only pay for your air ticket I'll also give you a cheque for a hundred pounds to help you get resettled. Of course the allowance would stop. I'm giving up this flat soon and where I'm going is no concern of yours."

"I'd crawl all the way on my hands and knees before I'd touch another penny of yours."

"As a penance, Mungo, that would be quite spectacular, especially if you went over the Pyrenees. Why put off? Why be beholden for another glass of wine? Wind the bandages round your knees and off you go. You'll have to consider whether it would be cheating taking the lift down."

Sadly, picking up the letter, he went into his tiny bedroom. There in the dressing-table mirror he gazed at his mournful, self-piteous, and yet still self-praising face. In his mind he saw another, not so familiar now, mournful too, worn with illness, but amused as always by the sight of his. And he remembered how once on the sands at Ettrick Bay, when he was on his hands and knees giving rides to Andrew and Peggy, Bess had plumped herself on his back, to the merriment of other parents round about. God help him, he had been proud then of that laughter and of the burden causing it, for at that time Bess had been happy and bonny, even if heavy for a woman. If she had since degenerated, so had he; and he was not so sure now that she had contributed more to his degeneration than he had to hers. He had perhaps blamed and punished her for inadequacies neither of them could help.

2

THOUGH HE HAD made up his mind to accept Myra's offer, increasing it five-fold if he could, and go back to Glasgow at any rate if not immediately to Minden Street, he kept pretending the decision was still to be made, with many frowns, sighs and groans. But before he went he was determined to find some compensation.

Ethne McGilvray was only too eager to provide it. Generous in breast and hough, with an earthy sense of humour not unlike Bess's, she was really far more his kind of woman than Myra. Still believing him to be well-to-do, she was just waiting to take him over.

The evening before his departure for Scotland it was all arranged. Myra had gone out and he was alone in the flat. When Ethne arrived he welcomed her in, kissing her hand as courteously as any Spaniard.

She was delighted. "No' bad for a dour Scot frae Glesca," she cried. Then she sniffed. "But he's been up to something more in his line: sampling the usquebaugh."

"Just enough to put him into the mood to receive as she deserves the beautiful lady in blue."

"D'you like it?" She turned round to let him admire the new costume. The skirt was short and very tight.

"Enchanting," he murmured.

She waggled her bottom as she went into the sitting-room where she sat on the couch, skirt hitched well up to reveal plump golden knees.

"And what would the beautiful lady in blue like to drink?" he asked. "Sherry?" He winked.

"Dinna be daft, Jock. Is this no' a foregaithering? Whusky, wi' watter; but no' too much watter, seeing it's no' genuine Loch Katrine."

As he poured out he said, "That's a bonny loch."

"To tell you the God's truth I've washed my backside, and other parts, in its water hundreds of times, but I've never seen it."

He hummed a Gaelic tune. "Yet yours is a Highland name."

"I didn't know you could sing, Mungo."

"I produce my accomplishments one at a time."

She had taken a sip of whisky when she caught his eye, found a thought in it that was also in hers, and began to splutter.

He patted her on the back.

"One at a time?" she cried. "For God's sake, don't frighten a woman. How many have you?"

"When I sing, I sing. When I drink, I drink. When I sign a cheque I sign a cheque. When I make love—"

"You make love. I find that most satisfactory. There are some who think they're sawing wood. But we forgot a toast. Shall we make it to Mungo's city, and may she always flourish?"

"To our city of leal and friendly hearts." He drank solemnly, then put his glass down on the tiled floor, far enough away to give him room to manœuvre. "Ethne, my dear, you and I are castaways this evening."

"Alas, on different islands."

"Within swimming distance, though."

"I'll be over in a minute."

"No, you must let me be the one to plunge in."

"There may be sharks, Mungo. You know what can happen to a man swimming in shark-infested waters. But I forgot: you've got more than one. So plunge in, lover, as soon as you like."

144

He eyed her lecherously. "On my island there are many trees laden with delicious fruits. One of them is love."

"Very delicious; goes well with whisky. But I bet it was never all that delicious with Myra. She's hard, isn't she? She always was, even at school. I bet she made you use a sheath, of double thickness."

She flung her arms round him and kissed him greedily, thrusting her tongue into his mouth.

Because she had the heart of a whore there could be no sin in deceiving her. No trust would be broken, no love dishonoured.

"We're wasting time," she whispered. "Just give me a couple of minutes." Grabbing her handbag she made for the bathroom. At the door she turned. "Meet you in bed, lover."

He went into the bigger bedroom, Myra's; yet it was with a curious reluctance that he undressed. He wondered if he was lowering himself with this lewd promiscuous woman. Once in bed he pulled the cover over his nakedness.

Ethne came in, utterly naked.

His eyes bulged as he saw the treat in store for him. Here was a Rubens' nymph. Her breasts, big and heavy, were supported artfully by an arm. As for the ample, soft, white, swelling, perfumed rest of her, he could find no fault. Beside her Nan Fraser was skinny and Myra a skeleton.

"Man, you're coy," she said, and pulled the cover off. "Let's imagine we're on a world cruise and that's the sea we hear outside, with flying fish and dolphins." She made a joke about a dolphin she had just seen.

Why, he wondered, almost in panic, had his predecessors at these large soft scented breasts, and in this deep golden groin, ever departed discontented? Here surely for any male was ecstasy and oblivion. Here, and only here, was the fount of joy, the source of peace, the cleansing of polluted conscience.

But it was not quite so. Her caresses were too purposeful, too lascivious, too fierce. Her legs entwined his, in a frenzy. Her great sponges almost suffocated him, and he was handled so rudely he might indeed have been drowning in a turbulent sea.

Then the door-bell rang.

"Christ," she cried, as she felt him go slack. "Let the bugger ring away, whoever it is. If it was Franco himself would you leave this for him?"

It couldn't be Myra back already; she had a key. The incongruous thought came into his mind that it might be nuns begging for some church charity. They had called yesterday and left an envelope.

But like a swimmer about to sink he had to go back to the love-making, and work hard at it.

After another minute or two the bell rang again.

This time he went so slack she had to let him go.

He muttered in his confusion it might be nuns.

She roared with laughter. "I'd say fetch them in and rape them, only it's my turn first; and to tell you the truth, lover, in spite of your boast a wee while ago I'm thinking I'm more than enough for you to be going on with."

Drawing on his dressing-gown he hurried to the door. Heart thumping, he opened it. No one was there. He heard the lift going down.

"Well, who is it?" yelled Ethne recklessly.

He went back to the bedroom. "They'd gone."

"Couldn't have been very important. Well, what are you standing there for? Don't tell me you're no longer in the mood."

Nor was he, but he had to pretend he was. Almost angrily, indeed painfully, she roused him.

"I don't like to do all the work, lover."

"Sorry." He tried harder.

"Here, what did I say about sawing wood?"

He wished that was what he was doing. Once in a cottage outside Rothesay one summer holiday he had enjoyed himself far more sawing a few logs for the fire than he was doing now. Bess had been in the house frying pancakes for tea. The children were playing on a swing he had improvised.

"Keep your mind on your work, lover," said Ethne, digging her long sharp nails into his back. She was heaving about as if demented.

His climax came and went without joy for him or tenderness from her. At her own wild consummation the telephone rang.

"Let the bloody thing ring," she yelled.

Beneath him her face was bloated and aged. In dismay he wondered where the elegant woman in the blue costume had gone, and the gentleman with the silvery hair.

He imagined Flo McTaggart standing at the foot of the bed. "So this is the way you raise the value of humanity?" she asked.

Ethne opened one eye. "Don't want to hurt your feelings, lover, but do you know what you reminded me of? A kirk elder misbehaving himself on the pew cushions with the minister's wife."

He tried to answer with dignity. "Kirk elders of my acquaintance are decent men, with daughters of their own."

She thought it was a joke and yelled with laughter.

The telephone still rang.

"Oh, go and silence that bloody thing," she said. "And bring me a drink. I think I've earned it."

Again wrapping his dressing-gown round him he went into the sitting-room and picked up the telephone. It was the portero speaking very earnest Spanish. Mungo could not understand a word. He called Ethne.

She came in still naked, and laughed at his shocked look. "It's not a periscope, you know." As she picked up the telephone with her other hand she flicked open his dressing-gown. "Poor Mungo, quite dejected. We'll have to do something about that. In the meantime get those drinks poured."

As she listened to the portero her grin did not die away but it changed.

"What's he saying?" asked Mungo.

She picked at her left nipple as she put the receiver down. "It's a telegram."

"Who for?"

"It's in English, and he doesn't understand English. So he's bringing it up. I told him just to slip it under the door. Now what about those drinks." She padded across to the sideboard.

He held her out a glass. His hand was shaking.

"Is your mother dead?" she asked.

"I never knew my mother."

She took a drink. "Then it must be your wife."

"Must be what?"

"Dead. That's him now."

The telegram was lying inside the door. He crouched down to take it out of the envelope and read its few curt words: 'Mother died today at three o'clock. Andrew.'

He saw Ethne's bare feet beside him, the toenails painted red. He remembered Bess's, particularly those on her pinkie toes, hooked, as she had said herself, like a Jew's nose. Often she had disgusted him by sitting in her nightgown snipping them.

Looking up he saw Ethne with a glass of whisky in one hand and a cigarette in the other. She stooped and took the telegram.

"Well, it's a blow," she said, "but it isn't as if you cared
148

for her any more. You're free now. That's one way to look at it. Who's Andrew?"

He kept shaking his head. He could not explain what he felt, he would never be able to explain to anyone. Most would blame him for having hastened his wife's death, and for having made unhappy her last few weeks of painful life, but thereafter they would shrug their shoulders and pass on. Nobody would wait long enough to be made understand.

Ethne touched him on the shoulder with her glass of whisky. "You're not so bad, Jock. You've got this, and you've got me."

He had never thought Bess would die. She would be there when at last, after a year or a lifetime, he returned to make his peace with her. In his absence, disciplined indeed by it, she would have mended her ways enough to be worthy of him again. Together they would end their days in reasonable friendliness. Their grandchildren would come, and he would be to them a wise good old man. But if Bess was dead, if she was at that moment smiling in her coffin on the sitting-room table, having displaced the brass pot with the artificial roses, if this really was her last joke, with himself as usual the victim, then that improvement and that reconciliation would never take place.

Ethne crouched beside him.

"Let her laugh," he muttered.

"Who's going to laugh? Myra?"

He took her glass and gulped down the rest of the whisky. Then it was so easy to topple her over, on her back. She laughed too, saying that the tiles were hard and cold.

3

IN DARK GREY fashionable Spanish suit, with the trousers narrow as trews, white shirt and silk tie, Mungo with a last wave to Ethne entered the plane, a Viscount of Aer Lingus, flying to Glasgow by way of Lourdes and Dublin. Myra's presents, gold watch and gold cuff-links, given him to buttress the pretence that he was a man of substance in his own right and not an escaped cave-dweller, gleamed in the morning sunshine as he practised the part he had decided to play, that of a rich business man, probably Canadian. Most buttressing of all, of course, was the cheque in his wallet. It was for three hundred pounds, to which sum he had wheedled Myra into raising it, with doleful tales about his responsibilities to his children and the difficulty at his age of finding a suitable job.

At Lourdes some Irish came on, one a cripple, and one obviously dying from some wasting disease. No miracle had been vouchsafed them. He studied their faces—"maps of Ireland" Bess would have called them—and sought in them reasons why divine beneficence had been withheld. They were heavy potato faces, all bumps and warts. A miracle would have been wasted on them.

Soon, however, he began to hate and fear them. They belonged to that part of his mind which he had dismissed. With their pain, disappointment, and above all their acceptance they reminded him that he would soon be home again in Glasgow where his cheating had begun and where it might be found out.

He sat in fear, imagining some official, uniformed like a

Customs officer and as politely persevering, asking him to show his sincerity, as if it was some kind of passport. He saw himself searching through baggage, pockets, wallet, soul, in vain.

Slowly he recovered. He was returning home. Glances at sincerity, as at passports, would be brief and cursory. There would be no inquisition, no suspicion of forgery. Even if his conscience was not clear there would still be no need to skulk. It would be understood that all consciences had hazy or dirty spots. The one person who might have had justification for questioning his credentials was gone; and she would have waived her right anyway. Therefore his position was strong. He need fear no man's and no woman's scrutiny.

At the air terminal in St. Enoch Square he was very confident as he took a taxi and asked the driver, in a Canadian accent, to take him to a good hotel.

Small, glum, assertive, the driver was a man who wanted only the truth. "Canadian or American, sir?" he asked.

"Canadian. Well, Scotch-Canadian. Canadian for the past fifteen years. Born here in Glasgow. I'm told I haven't quite lost the accent."

"It sticks through in places, but you can't help that."

"To tell you the truth I'm rather proud of it."

"Fair enough. But Scotland's finished, played out. You did the right thing getting out when you did, after the war. All the work and the money's gone south. They govern for themselves down there. Look at London. Things aren't as dear there, you know, as they're made out to be. Wages are higher, that's admitted, but then they'll tell you things are a lot dearer. Damned if it's true. My wife was there just last week, visiting her sister. Fruit, meat, clothes, all as cheap as here; often cheaper. We lie down to it too easily. If you'll excuse me saying it you and your kind that emigrated took the guts of the country with you."

Pleased and reassured Mungo gave him a tip bigger than the fare. "Would you be free about four o'clock this afternoon?" he asked.

"If it was worth my while."

"I think it would be. I was thinking of taking a drive through the streets where I was born and brought up. Out east-end way. Just a drive round. Could you manage that?"

"See you at four, sir."

In his hotel room Mungo took the telephone directory and made a list of funeral undertakers in the vicinity of Minden Street. Though he felt sure Alec Gilchrist and Son would be the firm given the business, he telephoned four others first, for the sad pleasure of putting off.

No, they told him, they weren't handling the arrangements for burying a Mrs. Mungo Niven of Minden Street. They were sorry they couldn't tell him who was, as there were dozens of undertakers in the city. It did not follow that a firm in the neighbourhood where the death had occurred would be engaged. Families often flitted from one part of the city to another but remained faithful to cemeteries and undertakers in the districts where they were born.

Very proper too, he gravely replied.

He knew old Sandy Gilchrist of Tobago Street. Stooped, crabbed, and yellow-skinned, he would have been dead long ago, so it was said, if he didn't grudge the expense of being buried by his own firm.

"Gilchrist and Son, morticians?" asked Mungo, in his Canadian voice.

"Alec Gilchrist, senior, speaking. Undertaker."

"I wonder if you could give me a piece of information, Mr. Gilchrist."

"In the way o' business, d'you mean? I'm nae free encyclopaedia. Who hae I the honour o' addressing?"

"It is in the way of business, I'm sorry to say."

"You hae a deceased?" The senile voice was shriller with interest. "You'll find oor equipment first-class, as guid as ony in the whole world, including America. A choice of Daimlers or Rollses. Prices as reasonable as ony in the city."

"I just want to know, sir, if your firm is handling the arrangements for the burial of a Mrs. Mungo Niven of Minden Street, some time tomorrow."

"It so happens we are. If it's juist a wreath you want to send, send it to the hoose."

"Is the burial in Janefield?"

"Aye. This is still an anonymous conversation on the one side, you ken. You havenae declared yet wha you are. You sound American, and I ken we're ca'd morticians ower there. I cannae say I fancy the name."

"When will the coffin be screwed down?"

"Now that's a private matter, Mr. Whatever's-your-name. I don't ken how it is wi' you Yanks but here we don't discuss sich things wi' every stranger that passes by. I tak it you are a stranger. Naebody said onything aboot Americans being among the mourners."

"I'm not a stranger, Mr. Gilchrist."

"Bess Niven never had a brither that went to the States as far as I ken. We're a firm, mister, that prides itself on keeping to schedule, not a minute lost or gained. The lid will be in permanent place at ten past two tomorrow afternoon. No one will look on the mortal remains after that."

"Thank you, Mr. Gilchrist. Much obliged."

He was smiling as he put the telephone down, but his hand was trembling. Bells had begun to toll far away in his mind. Old Gilchrist's greedy "You hae a deceased?" had set them going. They must be silenced until tomorrow afternoon when they might safely be allowed to ring for some minutes at the graveside. Otherwise how ridiculous to eat, drink, urinate,

153

sleep, and count his money, under the threat of their tolling. If they could not be stopped altogether they could at least be muted, or kept at a great distance, where they would be soothing to hear, and not disturbing.

The taxi-driver, on the way to the east end, past Glasgow Cross and along London Road, spoke feelingly about the passing scene, like a man still in prison to one set free. The place was improved, he admitted, but not all that much. Sure, institutions of horror, like the model lodging-houses for scabby old tramps, were now gone. Tenements of a squalor to make them notorious even here had been pulled down and decent enough flats built in their place. No women now, not even the old, wore shawls. Children were never seen barefooted. Buses had ousted those nuisances, tram-cars. You might claim therefore that there had been a sizable improvement. But what was the good of it if the taste had gone out of living in Glasgow, or in Scotland for that matter? He was seriously thinking of removing to London where his wife's sister's man had more or less promised to get him a job in a modern up-to-date factory that made sanitary towels. He turned quickly to stare at Mungo as he named the product, but found a face as sober and thoughtful as his own.

"You're the first I've said that to," he said, "that didn't snigger. Maybe like me you see the tragedy of it. There I've been offered up to thirty quid a week for making sanitary towels, while down at Brodericks in Clydebank where they used to make battleships they're either being paid off or lucky to get fifteen quid. They laugh. Me, I want to weep."

A dead woman did not need sanitary towels. Those were the absurd words the bells were now tolling, louder and harsher. In Barcelona he had schooled himself to remember Bess as a stranger and had succeeded well enough, for in many ways he had never known her. Now, though, as the taxi drew near to the street where she lay dead and where he had made love to her many times, he discovered that all those other intimacies, petty most of them, such as clipping her brassière at the back, nevertheless in their daily accumulation and repetitions had entangled him more inextricably than he had thought. There, for instance, was Finnie's fish and chip shop, to which he had gone when she was pregnant with Billy to buy her a fish supper for which she had taken a craving, though it would probably make her bilious and add to her fat. And there, God help him, was the little mysterious shop that sold among a host of other things coloured ribbons, baby's socks, safety-pins, knitting-needles, and sanitary towels. He had waited more than once at that cold corner while Bess was inside making her secretive purchase. "Nothing doing tonight, sweetheart," she had said when she had come out. As if there had ever been anything doing in the way of love.

The taxi turned into Minden Street. He asked the driver to go slowly, and then sat well back so as not to be seen.

"This where you first saw the light of day?" asked the driver.

"No. But I lived here for years."

"Some good properties here yet. Well-kept too. What number?"

Mungo told him. "But don't stop. Just drive past slowly."

"Sure. Why should you want to go through and see the wash-houses and coal cellars and the ground where you dug the holes for moshie? My wife's like that. The house she was born in, the places she played when she was a kid, the folk she knew, they're all marvellous. You spend your life looking back, I tell her. Me, forward every time. She's a bit of a joker too; she says that's a good motto for a taxi-driver: forward every time. This must be about it."

A black cat came very slowly out of the close, as if every

155

paw was rheumaticky. It was old Knox, still holding on. He was passed on the pavement by a woman Mungo didn't know, carrying a wreath.

"Good job you're not superstitious," said the driver. "A black cat and a wreath. Must be somebody dead. That's another thing, half the folk you knew as a kid are dead. My wife refuses to take that into account."

The blinds in the windows were drawn. Were Peggy, Andrew, and Billy sorrowing up there in that twilight? Or had they sensibly gone off to the cinema? That woman with the wreath, was she being taken into the sitting-room for a peep at the corpse? Was her conductress big fat blubbering Beatrice?

They passed the close and went slowly down the street.

"You lived in the prosperous part," said the driver. "Funny how you get streets like this all over the city, tiled closes and inside toilets at one end, and at the other dumps like these. I bet the folk back there don't let their kids mix with the kids here. Talk about the Berlin Wall. There's one here, though you can't see it. They're everywhere. Do you want me to turn and drive back, taking it easy?"

"Aye, do that."

"You know, sir, you said that as if you'd just left the place last week."

This time going along the street Mungo sat with his eyes closed. In his head those bells tolled intolerably. He could not bear to look out and see his old self walking the familiar pavements. That Mungo Niven had died and been buried months ago.

"Well, sir, that's it," said the driver, as they turned out of Minden Street. "In a couple of minutes you've left your past behind you. The best place for it. Where to now, sir?"

"Back to the hotel."

156

He lay on his bed for over an hour, listening to the noise of the traffic, which somehow was different from the Barcelona traffic. Shouts ascended which could only have been Glaswegian; one was by a woman who could have been Bess. He kept feeling at home, or about to feel at home, and he did not want to; or he thought he did not want to. He thought he wanted to be safe in the sunshine a thousand miles away. He tried not to remember that he had not felt all that safe there. In any case next time it was bound to be better.

The trouble was he could not be sure at any moment if he was the old or the new Mungo Niven. At times he was a confusing mixture of both. One minute he had made up his mind: tomorrow, skipping the funeral, he would fly off, to Italy this time, where he could draw courage from those great statues with the curly hair. Next minute he had made an opposite decision: he would go to the funeral, make his peace with Bess in her coffin, humble himself to her sister and brothers, and beg his children to give him a chance to atone.

That evening he telephoned to have a limousine and chauffeur, both suitable for a funeral, pick him up next day at a quarter to two.

So apparently he had decided: he was going to the funeral. Yes, but which Mungo Niven, the old or the new?

4

AFTER A MORNING spent wandering about the streets
and in and out of shops he still had not made up his mind
how he should conduct himself at the funeral that afternoon.
Ought he to go by bus or plain taxi, dressed soberly, without
any glitter of gold, a penitent, grateful for any scrap of forgiveness and sympathy, and in tears beside Bess's coffin
promising to make amends? There were attractions in such
a role, the chief being that it would demand no bold sequel.
Afterwards he would be able to stay at home with his children
and look for a new job. Myra's money could be honourably
returned to her, along with the expensive presents. He
would, in short, re-enter the ghetto; and if he was able to
convince its inhabitants that he was no better than they, then,
after a lot of gnashes and howls, they would take him back.
It would of course be at first a humiliating acceptance. He
would have to endure the insolent giggles of Nan Fraser, with
his head bowed, trying not to remember how he had had in
his arms the naked body of a woman far sexier than she.
Worst of all, he would have to suffer the ignominies heaped
on him like blows by that far more dangerous bitch, Flo
McTaggart.

There could be, perhaps, one advantage in playing care-
fully that humble role. One day when her small runt of an
Alec was out it was conceivable that he could slip upstairs
and enjoy little Nan on the black-and-orange striped sofa in
front of the fire. Even before his escape into the world she
had shown herself fascinated by him as a man who could give
her the gratification and awakening her Alec never could.

He became aware, standing in front of a counter in a big department store, that he had begun to let the one role develop into the other. So deep had he been in these thoughts that when he emerged from them he was astonished to find himself standing there by that cosmetics counter. The girl behind the counter, watching him, was artfully made up to advertise the products she was selling. Eye-shadowed, rouged, vividly lipsticked, and artificially blonde, she was more professionally whore-like than Ethne. Moreover, she was young, pretty, and shapely. He was about to smile back at her and then flee into the street. Instead, he began to chat gallantly to her about a birthday present he wanted to buy; he had thought of scent. Obviously impressed, she suggested names and fragrances. When she brought samples for him to see their hands touched, and he began to lust unbearably for her. He almost whispered his desire and need. Had he done so, probably she would have complained to a superior, police would have been summoned, and he would have been charged. Disgrace had been only a whisper away.

Furtively he bought a bottle of scent and slunk off.

The other role he might adopt was that of conqueror, who would invade the ghetto, in large gleaming limousine, overthrow it by his magnificence, and leave again, leading out those bold and spirited enough to want to be rescued. How grandly he would be able to play that part. Gibes and upbraidings would harm him no more than arrows a knight armed cap-a-pie. Mounted on his grandness, he would subdue all those carping, mean-spirited, visionless creatures, and by Bess's coffin reject, decently but firmly, the accusations in her dead eyes. He might even, making gasp those watching, bend down and place on her cold brow a nobler kiss than any she had ever allowed him to give her when alive. Let the whole ghetto howl its contumely. He would ride away, head high, the plume of self-esteem waving on his helmet.

The trouble was, ride where to? All very well to say Italy or back to Spain. It seemed to him, telling himself the truth, that there was no place where the dragon self-contempt would not reach to destroy him. On the other hand, if he went into the ghetto as one defeated and remorseful, he would be able after the ordeal was over to sit more or less peaceably at home, and by devoting his life to his children compensate for the wrong he had done their mother. Here too self-contempt would be encountered, but as a mangy old cat to be kicked out of the way, not as a huge devouring beast.

When the limousine called for him he still had not decided. Certainly the big opulent car belonged to the conqueror's role, as did his gold watch, gold cuff links, and dark red silk tie. But he could have the car stop before it reached Minden Street and walk the rest. The gold accoutrements could be put in his pocket.

As the car purred through well-known streets, nearer and nearer to where Bess lay, he became more and more agitated. It was as if like those Lourdes pilgrims he was expecting a sign from heaven. None was likely to come.

Just before turning into Minden Street he asked the driver to stop for a minute or two.

"I want to compose myself," he said.

"Very good, sir." The driver was young and well-trained. Gloved hands on the steering wheel he might have been praying. More likely he was considering how to fill in his football coupon for that week.

Mungo gazed out at the people of the ghetto, the shops where they made their careful purchases, the mouths of the caves where they lived.

After two or three minutes he said, "Please drive on now. Minden Street is the first on your left. No. 255 is about a third of the way down, on the right hand side. It's probable the hearse and coaches will be there already. Put me down as near the closemouth as you can, and then maybe you could take up a position at the rear of the cortège. Pick me up again as you pass. I have a right to be present but I want to exercise it discreetly. There may be some feeling against me. Do you understand?"

"Yes, sir. Clear enough."

"Good."

It was exactly two o'clock, ten minutes from the closing of the coffin. He shook his cuff links and straightened his tie. So he had decided to advance as a conqueror.

Had he not already made his decision when that morning he had sent a wreath, the biggest and most splendid in the shop? How after that magnificent challenge could he possibly have crept in, tail between his legs, like a stray cur whining for sympathy?

When they turned the corner into Minden Street he thought at first a house must be on fire, there was such a crowd. Most were women, and of course there was no fire, this was a demonstration. These women, sour-faced and middle-aged most of them, laid waste by years of ghetto marriage, had come out of their caves this pale April afternoon not only to pay homage to their dead comrade but also to demonstrate their undying hatred of him who had been guilty of worse than wife-beating or child-cruelty: he had escaped, leaving his wife behind to struggle by herself with all those drudgeries and pettinesses that made up ghetto life, and that had left them, after thirty or more years of it, haggard with the onset of the menopause and repellent sexually.

"The lady must have been well thought of," said the young driver, as he steered his car slowly through the mass.

"How do you know she's a woman?"

"Well, they wouldn't have turned out like this for a man, would they?"

Mungo sat well back. "You're young," he said. "You don't understand the world yet. If she had been a notorious murderess, who had killed her man and her children, would there not have been a bigger crowd than this?"

"Likely enough, sir. But they wouldn't have been crying."

It was no common sight to see public or even private tears on those grim, resolute, workworn faces. They read no books, appreciated no sculptures, saw no plays, and were more at home among lamp-posts than among trees. Their imaginations, lively enough in infancy, had long ago been starved to death. Where therefore did these tears spring from?

In spite of old Gilchrist's boast of punctuality the cortège was not yet outside the close, but even so there was an enormous crush of people there. Two policemen were trying to keep the closemouth clear but since they were young they did not like to order about so many fierce mournful mothers. They had, however, to push them aside respectfully to make room for the big black car.

Cries arose, of astonishment, indignation, affront, and something else not so identifiable: it seemed to Mungo that in spite of themselves they were impressed by his daring appearance.

"Who was she, sir?" asked the driver. "A relative?"

"The dead woman?"

"Yes, sir."

"She was my wife."

For a moment he studied the astonishment and surmise in the young man's eyes before stepping down among the women.

Their shrieks became intelligible.

"Christ Almighty, it is him, big Niven himself."

"Think shame, you heartless brute."

"Whuremaister."

"If I was near enough I'd scart oot your een, you big swanky bastard."

"Scart something else, Mary, that he thinks mair of than his een."

There was some laughter, very feminine and obscene.

The policemen looked at Mungo gravely, as if appealing to him not to expect them to be able to quell all those shouts, abusive though they were. He smiled back, to let them know he did not mind a bit.

At the closemouth, taking up a ringside seat as it were, was a woman he recognised, a Mrs. Murphy, who lived up a nearby close and about whose Irish mug and holy pictures Bess had joked with malice many a time. She put out her hand and held on to his coat sleeve, by finger and thumb, as if admiring the texture of the cloth.

"God forgie you, Mungo Niven," she cried. "She pined for you the minute you left. You could have saved her life."

He raised his hat and wished her good afternoon. Then he walked calmly into the close. It should have been very familiar, with every tile known and the place where Bess had stood that snowy night, returning with cancer from the whist; but somehow it was strange. Before he reached the stairs he thought he had discovered why: this narrow way had been for years the entrance to jail; every time he had gone through it he had felt there was no hope of escape. But this time he would soon be walking out again as calmly as he was walking in, and it would be for good. Glancing at his watch he saw he was slightly behind schedule. It was lucky Gilchrist's men were late. He did not hurry; inside the cloth, about whose expensive quality Mrs. Murphy would bore her neighbours for years, his legs moved smoothly, and his body felt warm and snug.

Three women passed him on the stairs, weeping. He did not know them, but they knew him: astonishment almost visibly dried their tears.

The door was open, no doubt to welcome those who wished

to say a last cheerio to Bess before Gilchrist's men came with the screw-driver. Women in black seemed to throng the hall. The hall-stand and the pegs on the board along the wall seemed to have sprouted men's hats. A good season for dark hats, he thought, as he hung his lighter one among them. As well as lighter in colour it was more expensive. One or two had sweat patches on the crown.

All doors were open, the sitting-room's, the living-room's, Peggy's, Billy and Andrew's; even the bathroom's. It was as if in superstitious belief about easy egress for the spirit of the dead. And of course the coffin too was still open.

In the living-room he caught a glimpse of men sitting, leaning forward, staring at their hacked knuckles, grunting, but leaving the business of audible grief to the women. Will and Dave, Bess's brothers, were among them; but he had already recognised their hats.

Out of the sitting-room, escorting big hairy-chinned Jean Aird, came, dressed in black, weeping or sobbing, Beatrice, Nellie, and Sadie.

When they saw him they did not look much surprised.

"So you've come," said Nellie, and shouted on her man, Will.

"I wonder you'd the nerve," said Sadie, more bitterly, and she shouted for Dave.

"Where's Peggy?" he asked. His voice was not as cool and clear as he meant it to be; there was a hoarseness and agitation he had not bargained for. He needed Peggy.

"She went out for a walk," replied Sadie, "and took Andrew with her. I'm not surprised it's her you're asking after. She's got more than a bit of her faither in her. Poor Andrew knew his place was here, but she would take him."

"Where's Billy?"

"Here." It was Will who spoke. He had come out of the living-room with Billy. He kept the boy in front of him, a

164

hand protectively on each shoulder. Billy was crying. At that moment neither Mungo nor anyone else could claim him. He was conscious only of the loss of his mother, and he wept for that so utterly he chilled all their hearts.

Except Beatrice's, it seemed. With a dignity Mungo had not thought her capable of, she closed the sitting-room door and then, arms folded, stood with her back to it.

"You're no' going in there to spit on my sister," she said.

"Now, Beat," muttered her husband Peter, "there's a time and place for everything."

Will and Dave, her brothers, were trying to decide what they should do. Anxious for peace, they still thought they should scowl sternly.

"Shut that ootside door, Sadie," said Dave. "This'll hae to be kept private."

"I'll shut it," said his small wife grimly, doing so, "though this day has been no holiday off work for me, Dave Aitchison. I've been up since dawn getting things ready. But as for keeping it private, how are you going to manage that, seeing there are some in the hoose that were never invited and haven't the decency to leave."

"I ken you mean me, Sadie," said a small sorrowful voice. "But I was invited. Peggy invited me. I've been keeping oot o' everybody's road. I juist wanted to be wi' Bess to the last. But if you a' think I should go then I suppose I'll hae to go."

It was Maggie Ralston, with a black armband round her dirty raincoat. She seemed to Mungo the one genuine mourner there. Everyone else, including poor Billy, missed Bess for something they had got out of her. Maggie's grief was strangely disinterested; and to his wonder part of it was for him.

"You made an awfu' mistake, Mungo," she said.

"If Peggy invited you, Mrs. Ralston, I want you to stay."

"Thanks, Mungo. I'd like to. But I'll keep oot the road."

165

Weeping she went back into the living-room.

Will had been conferring with Dave.

"We don't want ony unpleasantness at such a time," he said, "but we're inclined to think Beat's within her rights. You forfeited your rights three months ago. Aye."

"I still pay the rent."

As he had known, it was an argument that flummoxed them.

Sadie said, "Aye, but wi' whose money?"

"As one who wished you well in the past, Mungo," said Dave, "I'd say it would be better if you left us to get on wi' burying oor sister. Don't tell us she was your wife. She died telling us that. They were damn near her last words. But don't you tell us."

"Your wreath will represent you," said Sadie. "God knows it's big and flashy enough."

"It's not going on my sister's coffin," said Beatrice.

"Just one minute, please," said placid Nellie. "We shouldn't be squabbling in front of this poor wean." She went to the living-room door and called: "Will somebody look after wee Billy while we're settling an important piece of family business?"

Maggie Ralston came hurrying out. "I'll look after the wean, Nellie."

"The boy detests her," said Sadie, in a voice that nervousness, or spite, made too audible.

Nellie smiled, trying not to give offence. "Thanks, Maggie, but it'd better be somebody the wean kens weel. What about you, Nan?"

To Mungo's delight Nan Fraser appeared. She had on a dark blue dress that showed off the whiteness of her neck and the rounded softness of her body.

"Of course, Nellie," she said. "Poor Billy. You come with me." She put her arm round the boy and pressed him against

166

her. It struck Mungo as a provocation to him, and a challenge. He tingled to the ends of his moustache.

Then a loud knock was heard on the outside door.

"See who that is, Will," said his wife Nellie. "Don't open it till you know. It might be the minister or Gilchrist's men or just some nosy parkers."

"Dammit, Nellie, you know I'm a bit hard o' hearing. I cannae speak to somebody through a blank door."

"It's easy enough." She called, "Wha is it? Sorry the door's closed, but we're keeping it to the family these last few minutes."

"But it's us, Nellie: me, Jenny Stoddart, and Bella Martin, auld pals o' Bess's, sorry they're a bit late but anxious to say cheerio to the cheeriest lass ever trumped their aces."

"Sorry, Jenny. It's a family decision."

"We sent a wreath, Nellie. Could we speak to Beat?"

"Thanks for the wreath, Jenny. It'll be on the coffin. Beat's busy."

"Is it true big Niven's landed back? There's a whole street doon there fu' o' angry women."

"He's here."

"Would you credit it? If we're late, whit's he? But Bella here doesnae agree. She's a bit o' a spiritualist, you see, and she says Bess's spirit will be a lot happier knowing he came back before she was drapped oot o' sight. For we a' ken, Nellie, that though we miscalled him, wi' the best reason in the world, poor Bess never did. But talking through a door like this is like trying to get in touch wi' spirits. Bella's no' pleased wi' me, Nellie; she says I'm no' respectfu' enough. Weel, we'll be at the graveside. Tell big Niven that if he's got the brass impudence to be there we'll chuck stanes at him."

They turned away.

"There's nothing sacred," said Sadie bitterly. "I suppose you heard all that," she went on, to Mungo. "It was the truth she said about Bess never miscalling you. But don't you smile. It's nothing you can be proud of. Don't forget she was in terrible pain and often didn't know what she was saying."

Her husband Dave stared sombrely at the floor. "That's no' strictly accurate, Sadie," he said.

She was furious. "Are you calling me a liar to my face, in front of him, at a time like this?"

"I'm not calling you a liar, Sadie. I'm just suggesting that poor Bess knew very well whit she was saying when she was speaking aboot Mungo. We dae naebody ony good, and maybe we dae everybody harm, if we misreport her, even to him. But I certainly agree: it's naething he can be proud of."

Will asserted himself. "It's noticeable you've got little to say, Mungo. It's in your favour. Naething would be worse at this time than some o' that high-minded guff you used to sicken us a' with, aboot raising the value o' humanity. You lowered it worse than ony man I ever heard o'. You've come here and taken us at a disadvantage. I saw your wreath but I thought no man in your position would come in person after sending sich a brag o' a wreath. I'm no' a man of violence, unlike you I never was a sodger and killed nae men. Forby, you're bigger and heavier and younger. But I declare to God I'm tempted to crash this fist against your teeth. If you want to save us a' frae such indignities, go, for Christ's sake, and leave us in peace to bury oor sister."

Appalled, they listened to Will's sobs, and stared at him as he hid the nakedness of his grief behind a huge horny hand. His wife Nellie wasn't sure whether to be proud or affronted; she wept too.

Then the door was opened by someone with a key. It was Andrew. Peggy wasn't with him but Gilchrist's men were. He had been warned his father was there, and had decided how to greet him; this was with a big grin of welcome and an outstretched hand.

"Hello, Dad," he said. "I knew you'd come."

Mungo saw in him some of his own deceit. "Thanks for the telegram, Andrew. Where's Peggy?"

"She went straight to the cemetery. But what's going on here? What are you doing, Aunt Beatrice?"

"Can't you see? I'm not letting him in to gloat over my sister."

"But that's daft. You'll have to let him in. That's what he came for."

"If he couldn't come to see her when she was still alive, I don't think he can be all that anxious to see her now she's deid. Unless it's to gloat, and I'm no' going to let him do that."

Gilchrist's men had been pushed into Peggy's small room, but their presence in the house was urgent.

"So Peggy wouldn't come back?" said Sadie. "If you're going to tell me she didn't want to be here when the minister says his piece over her mother's remains then I'll be shocked but no' surprised. She's hard, is Peggy; far too hard for a young girl."

"Peggy can please herself," said Andrew, rudely. "She thinks," he explained to his father, "that since nobody really believes in eternal life it's a mockery to talk about it."

"So she's satisfied she'll never see her mither again?" cried Sadie, bursting into angry tears.

"She didn't say she was satisfied. All of you leave Peggy alone. She's got to get over this in her own way."

"Don't use that tone to me, Andrew Niven. I thought you took after your mother. Evidently not. I'm sorry for you."

"We're arguing in circles," said Peter, husband of Beatrice.

He had been begging her with his eyes to come away from the door. He could not see what difference it could make whether Niven saw or did not see his dead wife. Privately he agreed with young Peggy about the unlikeliness of eternal life; but in her case it was a bit early for so pessimistic a belief.

The door bell rang again. This time it was the minister, Mr. Brewster. Nellie let him in. As his policy was at funerals, he was briskly consolatory. Funerals that were too glum were not Christian, in his view; after all, the departed had gone to a better life. Neither of course were uproarious bacchanalias Christian, but these luckily had gone out of fashion. Here in front of him was a case of plain pagan glumness. So he thought and was about to dispel it with some brisk words of Christian encouragement when he suddenly noticed that Niven himself was present, the returned sinner, quite splendidly tanned and dressed in a suit that made all the other men, the minister included, look dowdy.

Mr. Brewster now noticed the atmosphere of hostility. This was not as rare on such occasions as it should have been. Often a death in a family was not the signal for armistice or truce, but rather for less merciful fighting.

He was relieved not to see that implacable little woman, Mrs. McTaggart. Where strife was likely to be engendered, there he would have expected to find her. Perhaps she had not come because he was officiating, just as she had told Mr. Peffermill there would be no wedding if the man who had tried to excuse Niven was to speak the words of union.

Here her role of troublemaker appeared to have been usurped by, of all women, that fat fushionless creature Beatrice Miller. Holding the door against Niven, she was exhibiting so much active ill-will the minister wondered from whom she could have borrowed it. Not from her husband who looked gloomily ashamed; nor from her brothers Will and Dave, solemn and glaikit respectively; perhaps from her formidable sister-in-law Sadie. But it could well be that the ill-will was Beatrice's own: it had just been buried deep in her soul under all the sloth.

They expected him to say something, to act as the referee

appointed by God. Sadie looked contemptuous. What her kind would respect was not of course possible. He could not slap sense into Mrs. Miller's fat obtuse face and haul her out of the way, thundering at her admonitions out of the Old Testament. Even more spectacular would have been a display of Christian moral force, miraculous in its effect; but that too was beyond his range. All he had at his command were a few threadbare exhortations to remember the solemnity of the occasion.

"If Christ was here," said Beatrice, "He'd be standing beside me. Don't tell me He'd be on his side?"

The minister appealed to her husband, the only man with any kind of right to slap and haul; but he indignantly shook his head. As a matter of fact Peter, who knew his wife's obstinacy better than any, was letting ridiculous thoughts scamper round his mind. If it was necessary for Niven to see his dead wife, couldn't it be arranged by Gilchrist's men down in the close, say, or even at the graveside, for of course Beatrice with the rest of the women of the family would stay in the house? Or alternatively, was there no other way into the room, up a drain-pipe for instance? Unfortunately the sitting-room looked down on to the street and hundreds would see Niven climb up; besides, his suit, which must have cost fifty pounds at least, would be ruined.

"You'll have to let Gilchrist's men in, Beat," whispered Sadie. "They say they're behind time as it is."

"Bess in there isn't short of time."

They all shivered. She had done what ought never to be done at a funeral; she had made them aware they themselves had only a limited time left, and here they were, as always, wasting it.

"But, Beat," pointed out Will, "it's oor time we've got to go by, not Bess's."

"To the end of the world," said Beatrice, cryptically.

They had all noticed how quiet Niven was. Either his silence was because he had nothing to say, or because, like his dead wife, he had plenty of time. He kept smiling, not nastily, but as if there was no need for him to smile nastily. He had more time than they, or thought he had, because he was superior to them, not on the strength of his fine suit and gold watch, which no doubt his wealthy trollop had given him, but because he was confident that when this squabble was over, with its revelation of their trivial-mindedness, he would go away again to where the sun had given him that tan, and where people were not provoked into being trivial-minded by rain, cold, and little sun; but even more by the necessity of too much hard menial work to keep bodies and minds respectable at least.

Thus they felt, each in his or her own way and degree, as they watched Niven smiling.

They would have been surprised had they known he was possessed by a great fear. He had always been aware that by leaving Bess and his children as he had done he had been guilty not only of adultery and betrayal, but of something more fundamental. What it was he had never tried to determine; through cowardice perhaps he had kept it hidden in his mind. Now, confronted by Beatrice, he saw it clearly, and was afraid. These faces, familiar, commonplace, and stupid, were suddenly seen to be nevertheless of great value, in a way he could never have explained; and any explanation would have been regarded by the minds behind those faces with suspicion and distrust, for in that vision of them he by no means bestowed on them qualities they did not have. They were valuable as they were, with all their imperfections; and the most valuable, to him, was now lost forever.

So for those few moments he saw; but he knew that, very soon, his mind dark again, he would despise them once more as typical creatures of the ghetto.

Suddenly, to everyone's astonishment, Beatrice wilted, and became her old, sobbing, fushionless self.

"A' right," she sobbed. "Go in and gloat. A big wreath, and no' even a black tie."

"Don't heed them, Dad," said Andrew. "They're just jealous. You know they've always been."

Sadie was the only one with enough spirit left to rebuke him.

"You're the right one to speak up for him, Andrew," she said, "you that's got that McKenzie girl in trouble and are washing your hands of it like a gentleman."

Andrew blushed. "Don't listen to them, Dad."

"When the wean's born," she went on, "we'll hae a good look at its teeth, and then we'll ken who its faither is."

"May I humbly suggest," said the minister, somewhat peeved, "that we go ahead with the business of the afternoon? Though it is true, as Mrs. Miller has reminded us, that we have only a limited temporal time still there should be ample for all we have to do, provided we have the good-will. Mr. Niven, the way is now clear. I would like to start the service as soon as possible, say, in no more than five minutes. That should give us all time to compose ourselves before we ask the Lord to take to His bosom our departed sister."

"That's been asked already," snapped Sadie. "Some of us don't have to wait for a dog-collar, you know. But whether it's worth asking, neither you nor me nor the Pope in Rome knows for certain. When you see the sort your Lord lets prosper it makes you wonder."

As Mungo slipped by himself into the sitting-room, he remembered, with overwhelming relief, that Peggy would be waiting at the graveside, not for any coffinful of dead hopes, reproaches, and bitterness, but for him, and Billy, and Andrew, who were still alive, and who, in spite of their failings which they would carry to their own graves, were her own flesh and blood, in need of her courage and honesty.

He had hoped that death, a far more practised cheat than he, would have removed from Bess's face every sign of suffering; that she would be as in her young days calm and bonny. But no, her face was heavy, dull, and old, and the pain of the last few weeks had twisted her mouth into a bitter version of her familiar grin. He could almost hear her whispering: "Well, Mungo, how do I look, lying in a date-box?" Coffins, she had once remarked, were like date-boxes, in shape, and with the white frilly paper round the edge.

He did not know what to say. Never had he been good at capping her jokes, or tempering them to the taste of any strangers who might be offended. Often she had laughed at his tongue-tiedness. "Be quiet, children. Your faither's trying to think of something funny." The result had been that in that mischievous silence the most brilliant of witticisms on his part would have sounded fatuous.

And so it was now, in this silence, in which he heard the beating of his own heart and the ticking of his gold watch. Bess, frequently so noisy, had known how to be uncannily quiet; but never before so quiet as this.

He wondered if he should bend and kiss her. Leaving aside its unavoidable impurities, would there still be in that kiss enough genuine love and grief to make it not too much of a fraud? It seemed to him she grinned at his hesitation. "Oot o' practice, Mungo? Surely no'."

There was a knock on the door. He straightened guiltily as Andrew looked in.

"Sorry, Dad. They're waiting."

"Let them wait."

Andrew came over. "There's nothing to say, is there? Just 'Cheerio, Mum, all the best.' Not much is it?" He began to weep and smile at the same time. "Look, Dad, this is really what I came in with." In his hand he held the little silver eagle. "Mum used to sit with this in her hand for hours. Peggy said it was her crucifix. I thought maybe it would be a good idea to let her have it with her."

Mungo took it. "Do you know how I got this?"

"War loot or something?"

"I took it from an old woman. To make her let go I hit her on the knuckles with the butt of my gun."

"An old Nazi?"

"An old woman."

"Mum wouldn't mind, Dad. You know how she hated the Germans."

"She's supposed to hate nobody now. Not even Catholics."

"I just thought it would be a good idea."

"Was she against Ishbel McKenzie to the end?"

"I'd rather not talk about that, Dad."

"Is the girl pregnant?"

"So she says."

"And does she still say you're responsible?"

"This isn't the place to talk about this, Dad."

"What place could be more suitable? Does she still accuse you?"

"Oh, sure. You know what they're like. Egged on by her mother, of course. *She* was out to trap me from the start."

"Are you responsible?"

"Look, Dad, this is my business. Just as what you did was yours."

"Suppose I admit that what I did was wrong?"

"That would still be your business."

"Why don't you admit it too?"

"I'll tell you why, though I think you already know. I don't intend to live up a close all my life. I saw what happened to you."

Then Will called from behind the door. "I've been sent to

tell you we're a' waiting. For my ain part you could stay in there till doomsday."

"We'll be with you in a minute," replied Mungo.

Andrew took the silver eagle and, with fumbling fingers, put it into his mother's hand. He took loud deep breaths to keep him from weeping. "There you are, Mum. He came back, as you said he would. Goodbye. All the best." He wept sorely.

"Goodbye, Bess," whispered Mungo.

In the hall they caught Will trying on Mungo's hat.

"I'll say this," he muttered, "it looks all right on you. But it makes me look an upstart, a foreman trying to be a manager. I'll never forgive you this side of the grave, Mungo Niven, but don't think I'm all that fond of the machine-shop myself. You were abroad?"

"Spain."

"Where they kill the bulls wi' swords. Aye."

Gilchrist's men came out of Peggy's room which they left full of cigarette smoke.

"All clear now?" they asked impatiently.

"Aye, screw her doon," said Will. "It's finished."

Then they went into the living-room to make it more crowded than ever. Within a minute Mr. Brewster had begun the service.

5

As MUNGO INVITED Maggie Ralston to go with him to
the cemetery Nan Fraser was nearby listening, and he found
himself wishing it could be her. Contemplating and smelling
her warm living perfumed flesh would have helped him to
forget Bess's, already rotting.

If he was not going to degenerate altogether into a sponger
and lecher, castrated of all ideals, he would need another
kind of help. Only from Peggy, he thought, could he get it.
In herself she was brave and inviolable, but she would also
remind him fruitfully of the days when as a young father he
had liked to push her in her pram or take her hand as she
toddled about. Surely she would be waiting by the grave,
with this gift of redemption.

The sight of the coffin and the multitude of wreaths, and
above all of Billy weeping, had calmed the women in the
street, so that when Mungo appeared, with Maggie courage-
ously beside him, he was greeted with grim silence, broken
only by sobs and an occasional yell from someone in the rear.
Guarded by a young policeman, he waited till his car came
along. Then he helped Maggie up into it, and climbed in
after her. As if they saw him escaping from their wrath the
women, now that the hearse was out of sight, began to shout
again, and this time they included Maggie in the abuse. Not
even her accepted weak-wittedness excused her this
treachery.

"I'm sorry, Maggie," he said. "I forgot."

"I didnae. I'm used to being thought daft."

Looking out, she caught sight of Mrs. McKenzie, Ishbel's

mother; her mouth was moving, in prayers or curses. I would like nothing better than to adopt the wean myself, thought Maggie; but nobody would allow it. Nivens and Aitchisons and McKenzies would all unite to say I was unfit, not able to keep even a goldfish alive.

"I was surprised not to see Florence McTaggart there," said Mungo. "Is she badly?"

"No. It was because o' Mr. Brewster. She's left his kirk, you ken."

"Why that?"

"To tell you the truth, Mungo, I think it was because he said a word in your favour. It's his job as a man o' God to find something guid aboot everybody, but Flo could never see that. I doot if we'll see her at the cemetery for the same reason. Latterly too, she was displeased wi' Bess. Flo, you see, can never mak allowances. She thought Bess should hae gi'en young Andrew and Ishbel McKenzie her blessing. She thought too Bess was unfair to young Peggy."

"In what way unfair, Maggie?"

She plucked shyly at her coat. He noticed a button was missing, and under her coat was a grimy apron. There was a smell off her too. After all, her house like so many in the ghetto had no bath.

"Pay nae heed to onything I say, Mungo. I'm just a daft wife that talks to the fly in her jam."

"I'd like to know, Maggie. How was she unfair to Peggy?"

"I wouldnae like to set you against the lass."

Shocked, and apprehensive, he muttered, "You could never do that."

"Bess, you see, would never hear a word against you. It aggravated them a', Flo especially. She never forgave poor Peggy."

"Who didn't?"

"Your Bess, Mungo."

"Why? What had Peggy done?"

"See, here I'm at it again. I just cannae help interfering in the business o' folk I like, even if, as is often the case, they're offended. But I'll tell you the truth. That's whit you came back for, to learn the truth. Wasn't it?"

"Aye."

"Weel, you see, Peggy blamed you for whit you did. She's never said it in as mony words to onybody, no' even to Flo, but it's been plain enough. Didn't she leave school to find a job because she wasn't willing to touch a penny o' your money? Bess saw it a' right."

"I was under the impression Peggy took neither my side nor her mother's."

"You cannae believe that, Mungo. Whit wrang did Bess ever dae compared to the one you did? Aye, Peggy blamed you, and Bess never forgave her for it. That's hard to believe, but it's true. Bess wanted everybody to take your side. Nae man in this world ever made a bigger mistake than you did, Mungo. Naething's worth mair than whit you threw awa'. Maybe you could still get some o' it back. There's still your family to consider, your weans, I mean."

He thought: go round begging for another job, work hard and humbly, and by restoring the fallen humanity in himself restore it in all.

Yes, and end up like one of those lonely old men in the public libraries.

"I'm nae Christian, Mungo, for I'm never inside a kirk frae one year's end to the ither, but I don't think you can expect no' to be punished for what you did."

They came in sight of the cemetery walls.

"Wasn't that a terrible thing Sadie said?" went on Maggie, with a sigh. "Aboot wee Billy detesting me. Whit is it aboot me that puts weans off? I offer them sweeties and they stick oot their tongues. They shout after me in the street.

179

Flo says it's because I'm too anxious to gie myself awa', like a kind o' present. Folk, she says, hae a sore enough job putting up wi' themselves. But I wad dee if folk didnae like me. I just cannae be as indifferent as a' these wi' the grass doors."

They had entered the cemetery, and were slowly following the coaches and hearse along the winding avenue. Those with the grass doors were the dead. Among them was Mungo's Aunt Kirstie. For a year or two after her death, when he was sixteen, he had visited her grave every Sunday afternoon and kept it tidy. Now it was quite forgotten.

"It's like an execution," said Maggie.

The car had stopped.

Looking out, he thought she ought really to have said a resurrection. All about were dozens of people, mostly women, standing by tombstones, and at the edges of graves as if newly risen out of these. Like neighbours everywhere they were looking with curiosity at the new grave, and the coffin as glossy as a chestnut that the bearers were now loading cautiously on to their shoulders.

Mungo did not go forward to claim a place.

With bare heads and devout spits on hands and earth, waited the two gravediggers, right feet on the shoulders of their spades, at a kind of attention.

It was a lucid afternoon, with patches of blue sky and clouds like pearls. Grass and granite glittered. Fresh daffodils lay on graves where grief was still fresh. In the distance the chimneys of the city smoked. The very worms in the soil must have been feeling the promise of spring. Mungo felt intensely what Bess had been deprived of. No worm or sparrow or human being had ever enjoyed life more.

"If you don't mind, Mungo," said Maggie, "I'll wait here in the car. My feet are sair. Besides, I like to greet alone."

"As you wish, Maggie."

He got out and walked slowly in pursuit of mourners and

coffin-bearers. Women whispered as he passed. One shouted
but her companions made her hush. He kept looking for
Peggy, more and more anxiously. His catching sight of her,
near the grave, coincided with the crashing of a heavy clod
on his back. There must have been a stone in it for it was
painful. Cries were heard, mainly of protest. He did not turn.
Some women called to some youths to put down the clods
they had in their hands. A policeman hurried over, not wishing to run in that sad place. As he passed Mungo he muttered
he'd soon get rid of them; he spoke guiltily, as if he felt
partly responsible.

Everyone had that look of being responsible, not just for
the clod thrown at him, but for the open grave, the coffin
about to be lowered into it, the many wreaths, Billy's weeping, Uncle Dave's half-blindness, the minister's untidy hair,
and for the betrayal of the dead woman.

Only one person seemed resolutely to refuse to accept any
responsibility at all; or so it seemed to Mungo. Bareheaded,
in a dark-red raincoat, Peggy watched everything and everybody, including him and the clod that had struck him, with
interest and intelligence, but without involvement.

He was unnerved. He wanted to shout: "For God's sake,
this is your mother they're burying. You shouldn't be standing over there among strangers. You should be here holding
one of these cords. To hell with that Scotch superstition or
taboo that says women mustn't. Don't you think you have a
better right than this clown beside me, your Uncle Peter,
who thinks he's comforting me and himself and your mother
who never respected him, by snivelling: 'Aye, Mungo, this
is whit we a' come to in the end, in spite o' oor squabbles'?"

Billy and Andrew held the same cord. Billy still wept.
Andrew kept patting him on the shoulder.

I am disqualified as a comforter, thought Mungo.

Very soon it was over, the coffin was snug in its lair, holy words and handfuls of earth thrown upon it. The minister put on his hat, Uncle Will blew his nose into his big white handkerchief, the gravediggers hitched up their moleskins, and the women crept out from among the tombstones to admire the wreaths and find out who had sent them.

Peter lifted his hand and knocked off some dirt that clung to Mungo's fine suit.

Andrew came discreetly over and whispered, "Where to now, Dad?"

Back at the house tea would be waiting. No steak-pie feast, Aunt Sadie had said, just cakes and biscuits. It had seemed a pity, for Bess herself had loved food.

"I mean," added Andrew, "I don't suppose you want to go back among that lot."

"What about Billy?"

Taking his Uncle Will's hand the boy was walking back to the coach in which he had come, still inconsolable.

"They've captured him," said Andrew. "I heard Uncle Will ask him if he'd like to go home with them. Not just for today either."

They walked slowly towards Mungo's car.

"And what about you?" asked Mungo. He kept turning to see what Peggy was doing.

Still standing by the grave, she must be in her own way saying good-bye to her mother. Was she now freely condemning him when Bess could no longer take his part?

"Well, I thought that might be up to you, Dad," Andrew was saying. "Are you staying in Glasgow for long?"

"I might be."

"Well, couldn't I just stay with you?"

"You bear no grudge then for what I did?"

"As I said, it was your business. I loved Mum and I'm going to miss her an awful lot. There's a great big hole inside me; I keep falling into it." He smiled, with tears in his eyes.

"But all the same I hope I've got more modern ideas than most of the folk who live around here. I don't intend to live up a close all my life, with ideas to suit. No thanks."

"And your sister, what about her?"

Andrew shrugged his shoulders. "She'll please herself. You know our Peg. As a matter of fact she's talking about going to America."

"America!"

"Some advertisement she saw in the paper. A job as mother's help. For a year. Since she's under twenty-one she needs your signature."

"Who does she know in America?"

"Nobody. That's why she's going. You know our Peg."

"Do I?"

"You're right there, Dad. None of us does really. Mum used to grumble about it. Remember? But I don't think she'll ask for your signature. She'll prefer to wait till she's twenty-one."

"Why shouldn't she ask for my signature?"

"You know her. Be beholden to nobody."

"That's a damned barren doctrine."

"Sure, but it's hers, especially nowadays. Ask her. Here she comes."

Mungo noticed the fresh clay on his daughter's shoes. Looking down, he saw it on his own. It seemed to be about all they had in common. Now that she was working for herself she was better dressed. He could hardly bear to meet her gaze. Her face was as pale and thin as ever. He noticed she now used lipstick. That touch of feminine vanity moved him greatly, and at the same time made him afraid. She was a woman now, able to assess just what he had done to her mother.

"Hello," she said.

He could scarcely trust himself to speak. "Hello, Peggy."

"It went off well enough, I suppose."

Her irony was harder to bear than all the others' animosity.

"Just the one clod, do you mean?"

"I was really thinking of Billy. Why didn't you speak to him?"

"I'm afraid I didn't get much of a chance. The Aitchisons have got him prisoner. The Nivens will have to rescue him, won't they?"

She did not answer.

He could think of nothing further to say himself. He read the inscription on a nearby tombstone: "Isabella Robertson, née Marshall, beloved wife of Archibald Robertson, and mother of Margaret and David, died 31st December, 1959." That must have been a hard Hogmanay for the Robertsons, whoever they were.

"Look," said Andrew, "it's daft standing out here when there's a big car over there empty."

"Empty?" Mungo looked for Maggie Ralston. She had stolen away. Only the young driver was there, chatting to two or three women who no doubt were letting him know just what kind of a scoundrel he had been hired by. "We might as well," he said. "We could go to some restaurant and have a talk over a meal."

"Good idea." Andrew made for the car.

Peggy stood where she was, shaking her head and taking from her pocket a piece of paper. "I'd be obliged if you'd sign this for me."

He took it. It was his consent to her taking a post in America.

"In case I decide to go," she said. "I haven't made up my mind yet."

"Andrew was telling me about this. Couldn't I just sign when you have made up your mind?"

"I might not know where to find you."

He made an offer then that surprised him. If she had accepted he would have forfeited his very soul trying to honour it.

"I was thinking, Peggy, that we could all keep together, as a family, I mean. It's what your mother would have wanted."

"You mean, in Glasgow? In Minden Street?"

"Well, to begin with, until we found something better."

"Which shouldn't be difficult," said Andrew.

But Peggy was again shaking her head. Thus his offer was rejected. Thus she was sending him into exile.

"I just want your signature."

And all he wanted was her forgiveness, pity, understanding, help, and love.

He took out his pen, the green one with the gold clasp that Myra had bought him.

Peggy was inexorable. "Use this one, please."

It was a ball-point pen costing no more than a shilling.

Disappointment profound enough to pervert his very soul made him see her as a skinny, callow, self-centred, would-be intellectual, of no comfort to any man's body or soul.

"For heaven's sake, what difference does a pen make?" asked Andrew.

They ignored him.

"I didn't notice Robert Logan about," said Mungo.

"I don't see much of him nowadays."

"Is he still sleeping with his red-haired librarian?"

"As far as I know."

"What's all this about?" asked Andrew.

Peggy was still holding out her pen.

Andrew snatched it. "I bet it won't write. She's got a dozen of these, Dad, in the drawer at home; all dried up." He tried it on his thumb nail. "Miraculous, it actually works."

"So you had your mind made up?" sneered Mungo. "Whether I came back or no."

"More or less."

"You're going to desert us in your turn?"

"If that's how you look at it."

"Suppose I sign this what do I gain?"

"What does anybody gain? Especially Billy."

"If you go to America you won't see him."

"No."

"Why go then? Why not stay here and help to look after him?"

She shrugged her shoulders.

"Peggy, maybe I deserve punishment, but it's not for you to inflict it."

"I'm inflicting nothing. I'm just minding my own business."

"I'll tell you what you're doing: you're banishing me. That's what you're doing."

"I don't think so."

"She's been seeing too much of Flo McTaggart," said Andrew.

"Suppose I refuse to sign this, Peggy, what will you do?"

"Wait till I'm twenty-one."

He tried to speak humbly. "Why are you doing this to me, Peggy?"

"To you?"

"Well, to us all. To Billy too. To yourself. If I sign will you at least stay with us until you go, if that's what you decide to do?"

"Isn't it too late? Billy's going to stay with Uncle Will and Aunt Nellie. Andrew's going to marry someone called Mary Daviot and live in a bungalow in King's Park. That's to say if you give him five hundred pounds."

Andrew went red. "Don't listen to her, Dad. She's just

186

jealous because she didn't get going to the University. And that was her own fault."

Again they ignored him.

"So if I sign this, Peggy, I shall sign the end of the Nivens as a family? Is that what you want? Is it what your mother would have wanted?"

"Please leave Mum out of it."

"You'll never forgive me, will you, Peggy?"

She did not reply, and waited for him to sign.

He signed, using her pen.

"Thanks," she said.

"Now that you've got your freedom," he said bitterly, "where are you going, if I'm allowed to ask?"

"Mrs. McTaggart's taking me in until she gets married."

"So she's marrying Peffermill?"

"In June."

"His wife's hardly dead a year."

None of them remarked his was dead only three days.

"A nice pair they'll make," said Mungo. "So, Peggy, you're going to take refuge with my bitterest enemy? Won't you get tired of hearing her run me down? Your mother used to."

"She loved Mum."

"No, she never loved anyone in her life. She's not capable of it. So she has made no mistakes."

Peggy said nothing. These silences baffled him.

"Well, will you keep in touch at least?"

"If I can. I'll write to Billy every week."

"And to me once in six months, if that?"

Again she was silent.

"You're not even asking where you should write to."

"I know the address, if it's the same one."

When he did not confirm it she said goodbye and walked away.

He murmured her name in bitterness as well as love.

"She's a crank," muttered Andrew. "Anti-bomb and all that stuff. She'll never be happy. Principle's more important to her than people."

Mungo could not bear the eager complicity in his son's eyes.

"Let's go," he said.

They went into the car.

"Back to the hotel, sir?" asked the driver.

"To the house first."

"Peggy's a spiteful besom," said Andrew. "I've never mentioned five hundred pounds."

"I hope not. Suppose you did have it though would you marry this girl Ishbel who's pregnant?"

"Not if it was five thousand. I promised Mum, you know."

"Just as well, for there will be no five hundred pounds, I'm afraid."

"I did think I was entitled to something."

"Share of the loot, eh?"

"You know I didn't mean that."

"Why didn't you? For that's what it would be. Didn't I see tears rolling down your cheeks a few minutes ago?"

"I loved Mum."

Mungo nodded, not surprised that venality could consort with grief.

In another two or three minutes they would be at the close-mouth in Minden Street. What was to be done with the loot that was left? Use it for the purpose Myra had given it for, helping him and his family to resettle in the ghetto? Or spend it on a glorious trip to Italy, say, where, who knew, love and adventure were waiting near the great curly-haired statues?

Let Will and Nellie have Billy. Let Andrew marry this University girl-friend and buy a bungalow in King's Park. And let Peggy learn humility and forgiveness by looking after some rich American's spoiled brats.

No, he could scarcely be expected to come tamely back to Minden Street and set up as an aproned widower, running to the door with a half-dried plate in his hand every time he thought he heard Nan Fraser come down the stairs.

The car stopped. They were at the closemouth. Andrew had been talking, his teeth very earnest. Mungo had not heard a word.

"Well, my boy," he said, "it's goodbye again."

"You're not coming up then?"

"No." He brought out his wallet and from it took a five pound note. "Take this, in the meantime. I'll write. Keep an eye on Billy."

"What about that fifteen quid for the car trip, Dad? I said I'd go. I can't very well back out now."

Mungo again produced his wallet and reluctantly took out two more five pound notes. "Make this last," he said.

"But what about the allowance? I suppose it could be reduced. Ten pounds might do. Till I get a job as a teacher, next September."

Mungo hesitated, not willing to lie too callously. "We'll see. Things have changed, you know."

"Yes. I've been wondering, Dad, if you would get married again. Like wee Peffermill."

"It's possible."

"Dad, if Billy's staying with Uncle Will and Peggy with Flo McTaggart, and I'm out at King's Park with Mary's people, what about the furniture in the house here? Should I just go ahead and have it sold?"

"A good idea."

"I'd share the money with Billy and Peggy, of course."

"That would be only fair."

"Not that it will amount to very much. I mean, most of the stuff is old. Is there anything you'd like, Dad, as a souvenir?"

"Nothing that I can think of."

"Will the same address reach you?"

"No, it so happens it wouldn't. I'll write."

"I'd better let you have my address."

Then to Mungo's delight who should appear at the close-mouth but Nan Fraser. He put his head out of the car and spoke to her in a voice that, though deep and sorrowful, also suited his expensive clothes, his rich man's tan, and the gold watch.

"Good afternoon, Nan. I'm sorry to say the snow has all melted from those trees."

She pretended to be annoyed, but her frown, and blush, and sly little orange-hued smile really indicated pleasure.

"Just saying goodbye to Minden Street for the last time," he said.

Though she kept frowning she did not hurry away. "Are you going back to Spain?"

"Italy this time."

"We've been to Italy," she said, unexpectedly.

"Ah, those magnificent statues in the sunshine, Nan."

"I'd just as soon have Glasgow," she said, blushing again. Then off she went, with her dainty little buttocks vexed.

He took his head into the car, to find Andrew handing him a piece of paper. On it was written an address in King's Park.

"Who are these Daviots?" he asked.

"Mary's in my class at Varsity. She's going to be a teacher too."

"What does her father do?"

"He's a teacher."

"I see. So it's goodbye to Ishbel McKenzie?"

"I told you I promised Mum."

"So you did. Well, Andrew, when you go up there among them remember you're my representative. Hold your head high. Don't let them turn you into a cave-dweller."

"They'll never do that."

"Good. Work hard at your studies. Do well in June."

"Will you come to see me capped?"

"I'll make every effort."

Reluctantly Andrew got out. "You'll be sure to write, Dad?"

"Never fear. In the meantime, the very best of good wishes."

He nodded to the driver, and the big car slid quietly away.

As Andrew stood staring after it a girl went hurrying across the street towards him. She had fair hair and looked desperate. When he saw her he bolted into the close. What she did then Mungo could not see for the car turned a corner. Lighting a cigarette, with a hand that shook ever so slightly, he settled back to think of Italy or some other beautiful place of banishment, where with luck he might find another Myra, richer, more passionate, more amenable, and more faithful.

POLYGON is an imprint of Birlinn Limited. Our list includes titles by Alexander McCall Smith, Liz Lochhead, Kenneth White, Robin Jenkins and other critically acclaimed authors. Should you wish to be put on our catalogue mailing list **contact**:

Catalogue Request
Polygon
West Newington House
10 Newington Road
Edinburgh EH9 1QS
Scotland, UK

Tel: +44 (0) 131 668 4371
Fax: +44 (0) 131 668 4466
e-mail: info@birlinn.co.uk

Postage and packing is free within the UK. For overseas orders, postage and packing (airmail) will be charged at 30% of the total order value.

Our complete list can be viewed on our website. Go to **www.birlinn.co.uk** and click on the Polygon logo at the top of the home page.